The Oyster Diaries

BY THE SAME AUTHOR

The Fiery Pantheon

Lives of the Saints

Malaise

The Ritz of the Bayou

Sportsman's Paradise

The Oyster Diaries

A Novel

NANCY LEMANN

nyrb New York Review Books New York

This is a New York Review Book

published by The New York Review of Books

207 East 32nd Street, New York, NY 10016

www.nyrb.com

Portions of this work have previously appeared, in slightly different form, in the following: "Diary of Remorse" was first published in *The Paris Review* (Issue #241); "The Oyster Diaries" was first published in *The Paris Review* (Issue #248); "Lions and Daughters" (copyright © 2023 by *Harper's Magazine*, all rights reserved) was first published in *Harper's Magazine* (June 2023) and is reproduced here by special permission.

Library of Congress Cataloging-in-Publication Data
Names: Lemann, Nancy author
Title: The oyster diaries / by Nancy Lemann.
Description: New York : New York Review Books, 2026.
Identifiers: LCCN 2025035057 (print) | LCCN 2025035058 (ebook) | ISBN 9798896230328 paperback | ISBN 9798896230335 ebook
Subjects: LCGFT: Diary fiction | Novels | Fiction
Classification: LCC PS3562.E4659 O97 2026 (print) | LCC PS3562.E4659 (ebook)
LC record available at https://lccn.loc.gov/2025035057
LC ebook record available at https://lccn.loc.gov/2025035058

ISBN 979-8-89623-032-8
Available as an electronic book; ISBN 979-8-89623-033-5

The authorized representative in the EU for product safety and compliance is eucomply OÜ, Pärnu mnt 139b-14, 11317 Tallinn, Estonia, hello@eucompliancepartner.com, +33 757690241.

Printed in the United States of America on acid-free paper.
10 9 8 7 6 5 4 3 2 1

Contents

To Emmeline & Eliza
And to the memory of my father

You won't find a new country, won't find another shore.
This city will always pursue you.

—C. P. CAVAFY

All the business of war, and indeed all the business of life, is to endeavor to find out what you do not know by what you do. That is what I called guessing what was at the other side of the hill.

—THE DUKE OF WELLINGTON

Diary of Remorse

I WAS PLAGUED by remorse, but my remorse seemed inspired by insignificant dumb things—things not really worthy of bona fide remorse. That didn't make it any less painful or plague-worthy, as I was still riddled with disgrace on a minute-by-minute basis; so I decided to conduct a scientific study to analyze the cause.

Remorse is akin to regret but more violent than regret. The overall atmosphere seemed like generic self-loathing. But that was too vague. Once I conducted the scientifically controlled study, I could identify the source of the trouble and modify my behavior so I would not be covered in dishonor.

It was a Wednesday morning in our nation's capital. The president's helicopter flew overhead, rattling the windows of my house. The world's handsomest man, who lived across the street, was listening to opera in his garden. Supposedly he worked at the National Security Council. So why was he listening to opera in the middle of the day wearing his gym shorts? Probably a spy. But the opera was significant.

That night I went to *Rigoletto* at the neighborhood movie

theater where they stream productions from the Royal Opera House in London. I had no real expectations because usually in their presentations you have to watch these super annoying blond-haired women in evening gowns effusing in an airhead way about the opera for what seems like an eternity before it starts. You have to grit your teeth to get through that—and then they do it again at intermission. Plus between the acts. Even their erudite-sounding British accents cannot rescue these breathy blond-haired women in ball gowns from their realm of being incredibly annoying and idiotic.

But they didn't do it that way this time—maybe they got too many complaints about how excruciating it was. Instead they had the conductor making scholarly points about the opera: the comic and the tragic alternating, the ridiculous preceding the sublime. As in *Don Giovanni*.

The duke must have reminded me of Don Giovanni, for I could not stop thinking of him. His love of life, his hopeless philandering, the robust way he throws his voice into its registers, the effort visibly emanating from his physical frame. I was ecstatic—to be moved by something, to feel, to think, and to remember.

A return of my old obsession with *Don Giovanni* consumed me. I found a new production of it to stream on my device when I got home—noting that its star, Erwin Schrott, was the same one who had played the role twenty years ago when I first moved to Washington, DC, and attended the opera here. He had struck me deeply at that time. He was young then, I remember noting. I marveled at his youth. He was twenty years younger than me. Now he would be twenty years older—as would I. So this would be a profound rotation.

And there was an additional rotation from twenty years before that, when I first became obsessed with *Don Giovanni* and studied it endlessly on the screen porch of my apartment in New Orleans, while the streetcar rumbled past.

The philosophical idea of the rotation often comes up in the novels of Walker Percy, the hero of my youth. Walker Percy seemed to have got the idea from Kierkegaard and then run with it in his own way. I would have to pursue the original rendition of the concept to seek more understanding of its elusive meaning.

Kierkegaard was so not what I expected. I started at the beginning. First he keeps talking about how boring and annoying everything is. "It is a curious fact that those who do not bore themselves usually bore others, while those who bore themselves entertain others. Those who do not bore themselves are . . . the most tiresome, the most utterly unendurable."

Many fine points about what is annoying and boring follow. "The unpleasant is merely a piquant ingredient in the dullness of life."

Which explains why it is so diverting to analyze things that are annoying.

So far Kierkegaard was everything I adore: he's in a bad

mood, everything annoys him, and he is not afraid to repeat himself. Kierkegaard was my bible, my blueprint, it was turning out. And it was all leading to the key issue—the Walker Percy rotation or Kierkegaardian repetition.

Which I would apply to the Erwin Schrott–Don Giovanni situation.

"It is in your power to review your life, to look at things you saw before, but from another point of view."

Erwin Schrott playing Don Giovanni: Was it the same or different twenty years ago, and if so, how?

Or rather: What is different, among the circumstances of the thing itself that is the same (*Don Giovanni*)? The thing is the same, but you are different?

A friend of mine in New Orleans claims to remember everything he's ever seen or been told. Remembers everything that used to be everywhere where something else is now. A lot of it was his father showing him things when he was a boy. He lives two blocks from where he grew up, assailed by his memories at every turn.

Mildred, his nurse, who weighed three hundred pounds and always stored her gum behind her ear. The Cannibal Special at Camellia Grill. How there used to be hat racks everywhere. His grandfather wearing a straw boater hat and a seersucker suit wobbling toward him while he was playing with his friends in the street.

"Would you kids like a cracker?" said his grandfather.

"Henry get back in the house," yelled his grandmother.

At night listening to the train whistle blow and the lions roar in Audubon Park. Weenie Bradley, who drank herself to death the night before her daughter's wedding. The mental institution between Magazine Street and Tchoupitoulas in a dark moss-hung quadrangle next to the Home for Incurables. The gray days, the twisted oaks. Near the levee next to the insane asylum.

"The past is so much a part of the present here and it's unhealthy," my friend says.

"The passage of time upsets him," says his wife.

"OK, but the passage of time upsets everyone," I said.

That bend in the river, where the hospital is—my mother died there, I was born there.

According to Kierkegaard, "It is a very beautiful sight to see a man put out to sea with the fair wind of hope . . . but one should never permit hope to be taken aboard one's own ship, least of all as a pilot; for hope is a faithless shipmaster."

Or to summarize: Only when you cease to hope are your hopes realized.

February 1, 2021

First day of scientifically controlled study

No remorse, shockingly.

Twenty years ago when I moved to Washington and went to *Don Giovanni* I did not know that I was destined for a decade of increasing heartaches culminating in a bonanza of heartache that ultimately calibrated my soul with insight my soul had been waiting for its whole life. I had never understood the adage that failure and despair can be elucidating and strengthening. All that was unbeknownst to me then.

I took the subway downtown. The weather was gray and cool. Helicopters flew overhead. America had invaded Iraq. I was paranoid. The streets were curiously empty. Washington is a strange town to get a handle on. It's a more small-time town than New York. But I have a love-hate relationship with New York now, for its atmosphere of a dying civilization, a decaying frazzled edifice that could easily crumble and crash to an end. The love part is for its suave crumbling gleam. Same with New Orleans—which is ever more rickety than suave.

Washington is not the type of place that reaches in and grabs you by the heart and makes you fall in love with it. Government and politics and pundits—you don't fall in love with that. Unless you're already in love with that. And the capital, despite its immense officious buildings and gleaming infrastructure to protect the pols, certainly had a sinister air at that moment, when we had invaded Iraq.

The cherry blossoms were duly out in the cool gray evening. Cherry blossoms don't ordinarily grab me but I will admit they looked nice. Giant pandas don't really grab me either, even though everyone is constantly raving about how adorable they are. There were no cafés to stop at as I proceeded on my way to the opera hall. That's the nature of this town—all business. Methodical, plodding, no cafés for boulevardiers and bohemians. There are no bohemians or boulevardiers in Washington. So I just sat and read for an hour in the hall, being early.

I did not know when I had heard such beautiful singing before. I wept silently for the duration of the performance. Don Giovanni in particular had the most beautiful voice. But the shock at first was how young he was. How young they all were. I had never seen such young opera singers, surely. It meant of course that I was now old. But this wasn't depressing. It was actually exhilarating. There's a feeling that the young have their battles to fight and dreams to achieve and you have already fought and achieved yours. But what then?

Usually the opera is in a vast hall with a vast remote stage and the actors in a stiff tableau. This time I was sitting in a box right on top of the stage in a quaint historic building because the Kennedy Center was being renovated. A lucky break because I despise the Kennedy Center, with its soul-crushing Soviet-style architecture.

In the production notes it said that the director of the Washington Opera, Plácido Domingo at that time, wanted the locale to seem like Seville. And indeed it did. It also reminded me of Palermo, maybe because I was reading a biography of Lampedusa with its hypnotic cast of ruined aristocrats paralyzed by centuries of decadence. Sun-bleached squares and café tables and white umbrellas and processions of priests and popes and bishops. The young man who played Don Giovanni—Erwin Schrott—did overact a bit, but no overacting could detract from the sheer beauty of his voice. I could not understand how such a young boy could have such a voice. I had never heard a bass like his. In one scene they had him take off his shirt, and that was very poignant. I just wanted to end my life and go off with him.

I was glued to the stage, weeping silently at the beauty of the entire evening. It made you forget the war in Iraq for an hour or two, getting lost in the garden of art.

"My soul always turns back to the Old Testament and to Shakespeare," says Kierkegaard.

"I feel that those who speak there are at least human beings: they hate, they love, they murder their enemies, and curse their descendants throughout all generations, they sin."

Also they get depressed. Like the guy at the beginning of *The Merchant of Venice* with the random melancholy. Kierkegaard was definitely getting depressed as I read on. Sinking into lassitude, boredom, etc. "My soul has lost its potentiality." He goes on and on about it.

He keeps getting more depressed and annoyed by everything. Until suddenly—someone is trying to tell me something—for the next sentence is: "What do I hear—the minuet from *Don Giovanni*!"

(Are you kidding me?)

3 p.m. still no remorse

February 2, 2021

However I did get a sinus cold yesterday. I think it came from the movie theater where I attended *Rigoletto*, which was filthy, as if it hadn't been cleaned in a year, as is probably the case, due to COVID—no revenues, skeleton crews, etc. It was permeated with the kind of mold or bacteria that could get into my sinuses and cause problems. Not only that, but I had to have emergency dental surgery.

My dentist and I have a unique relationship. A sadomasochistic relationship, maybe. She has an interesting attitude to dentistry. Other dentists have fancy staffs and high-tech equipment. My dentist is more like Ernest Shackleton. Modern innovation in dentistry is not her focus but she gets the job done.

The sinus and dental problems come with a psychic or spiritual malaise: I have no thoughts, no personality, nothing. "My soul has lost its potentiality," as Kierkegaard would say. And even though I can't help but notice that he devotes virtually an entire book—or at least several dense chapters—to the bliss inspired by *Don Giovanni*, I can formulate no thoughts about them, and it is all because of my sinuses.

Also you don't expect bliss from Kierkegaard, so it's disconcerting.

Now he's back on his home turf: how boring everything is. Ironically that is the least boring part. To see him careen from the heights of bliss back to his depression and boredom—it's like watching the World Series waiting for that final archetypal moment where the winners go berserk with joy on the field and the losers stare vacantly in the dugout.

February 5, 2021

Ever since I started keeping my diary of remorse, my remorse has evaporated.

The lockdowns start and stop and then I go back and forth to my odd and unlikely hometown. I see that my interest in my volunteer job (monitoring justice in New Orleans criminal courts) is largely prurient. For this I should have remorse but don't. When I get my docket in the morning I compare it to all the other dockets, pining that they are more exciting. Judge DeBose has murders, rapes, and kidnappings on his docket today, not to mention a case of false personation (???) and false imprisonment, but I am not assigned to his courtroom. My consolation however is that today I am in the courtroom of the piping mad personality-ridden Judge Hollingsworth.

The defendants in New Orleans always have names like:

Jockward Jones

King Malveaux

Stokes Meilleur

Bingo Fox

Margaret Lemmonier

And the judges have names like that too. Talk about a vanished world. The grandiose criminal court building. The old-time bars and cafés amid the greenery.

February 9, 2021

A smooth flight in, despite a storm, the swamps in darkness, the pavement glistening, a black sky, palms. The Gulf South.

The curtain rises. The tragedies begin.

The stated context of my work is to observe/monitor/report injustice. I am an observer, officially, who has not observed any bad judicial conduct or impropriety in any legal proceeding; the only improper thing I have observed is the overall shock of how things are there: almost 90 percent of defendants are black. (85 percent of the judges are now black, at least, on the plus side.)

Judge Hollingsworth was very calm today. Everything was running smoothly. I guess that's why she was calm. Usually she's piping mad. There's a lot for Judge Hollingsworth to get mad about: Mardi Gras delays, no-show lawyers, huge backlogs from COVID. She wants things to move along. Complains that everyone is wasting her time. On the warpath.

She had thirty-nine cases on her docket today. She wants New Orleans police officers testifying in court to get back out on the street protecting the public. She has cases that have dragged on for two years that she is incensed about. She denied a bond reduction. She keeps giving everyone these withering looks. Kind of like Chef Ramsay.

Murder trials every day upcoming, due to the backlog from COVID. I see that Judge Hollingsworth has the bulk of them. She is the chief criminal court judge.

February 10, 2021

Kierkegaard's unexpectedly boring one-hundred-page discussion of *Don Giovanni* prompted me to search for my own lengthy study of it, the one conducted on the screen porch on St. Charles Avenue when I was twenty-three. I know where it is.

Then again, I knew where the diary of my mother's funeral was. And it wasn't. I took notes at my mother's funeral in a small blue-and-white notebook. Since then I always knew exactly where it was—being a precious item of key importance, I kept it in a highly visible and accessible place. I often saw it. But when I searched for it the other day for hours, it was nowhere to be found.

February 11, 2021

Judge Hollingsworth has forty-two cases on her docket today and twenty-five of them are murders.

Lawyers missing. Boy is she mad. Always at the end of her rope. Indeed it would be hard not to be. I have seen how other judges handle it: they are just calm and congenial and accept that this is how it is. "It's the story of Section K—waiting for the lawyers," says Judge DeBose. That's the story of every courtroom as far as I can tell.

I do find it refreshing to encounter Judge Hollingsworth's opposite mode: on the warpath. Her technique is to call the docket and if no one's there, tough luck.

Of the twelve criminal court judges, ten are black, and most of those are black women.

Black women are by far the best judges. Because they've had

it up to here and they don't have time for falderal. Like Judge Hollingsworth.

Mardi Gras scheduling conflicts annoy her greatly. Lawyers also annoy her. She doesn't like the police either. Everyone is sort of quavering in fear of her.

She is protective toward the defendants.

"I'm tired of going to jail," said an incarcerated defendant.

"We're tired of putting you there," said the judge.

There was a juvenile rape case. No plea deal. They were at an impasse on the case. She set it for trial, maneuvering between her other rape cases so that they would be on different days: "I can only take so much sex in one day."

A public defender in a domestic abuse case was missing. "He's in a murder trial down the hall," said his colleague (the young handsome one with long hair—looks like Don Giovanni), whom he had authorized to stand in. The judge asked if the defendant was a multiple offender; the stand-in PD hemmed and hawed—like Ed Norton in *The Honeymooners* shooting his cuffs to procrastinate before executing a task. Just answer the question, Yes or No, said the judge.

The DA recommended ninety more days in the domestic abuse intervention program. The stand-in PD said he didn't feel comfortable with that.

It was at this point that the judge's patience began to fray. She had thirty-five items on her docket scheduled for Wednesday already, so she didn't really want to reset this case. But she had to, owing to the unflinching ideals of the romantic long-haired stand-in PD, who would make no concessions in his quest to protect his client from censure.

Things came to a standstill after that because of all the no-shows, and she took a recess. So I watched the new production of *Don Giovanni* on my device, comparing it to the one I'd seen twenty years earlier. The star, Erwin Schrott, was no longer a stick of a boy. But he still had the magnetic allure of the Don. He was maybe more sedate. Middle age? No, that has nothing to do with it. Don Giovanni could be middle-aged and still ravishing. Dialing it in? Not exactly. More like the spark of divine fire burned slightly more dimly, on its inexorable path toward decrepitude and extinction. He still had the same resounding bass. It was still gorgeous. It still emanated from his entire body and his entire soul.

The ultimate rotation may be that the Don is the same but a million different opera singers play him through the centuries, variously altering his persona. Erwin Schrott has an innate elegance and grace that some lack and if they lack it then the Don can be creepy. I don't think that is the true spirit of the thing. It's meant to be that you adore him and he is bad; you adore a bad thing.

They changed the end, when the Don is swallowed by the

inferno of hell. Instead they made him cower in fear alone on the stage for five minutes. It is not in Don Giovanni's nature to cower. He does not have a cowering soul.

Otherwise the essential thing remained the same. The essential thing being that he is a heartthrob. The cad we have all been ravished by who always breaks your heart, but he makes your heart beat faster. Otherwise it would be a boring morality play.

Yes in the end he is punished, but some of the boring moralizers heralding his downfall are subtly skewered, and there is a giant hole in your heart where he was before. You miss him.

The last time I saw Walker Percy, who lived across Lake Pontchartrain in Covington, a giant storm was rolling in over the bridge—the longest bridge in the world—that I would be driving on to get back home. We looked out at the gathering storm and he said, "Delery, the next half hour is going to be good for your soul."

Because fear is good for the soul? The way despair can make you notice things more? That is the whole point of everything—to notice things more. But I don't know exactly what he meant, as I suspect his comment had a religious connotation; he was a zealous Catholic convert. Good for the soul, as in the bracing fear of the wrath of God? Or when you think you are lost, salvation is near?

Impressively ominous and dramatic and threatening cyclone- style vast black clouds were forming, which somehow

I was able to note philosophically and absorb the beauty of—despite being about to drive into them. Maybe that's what he meant, to face a trial, to meet what comes. But I don't really know.

What I do know is that he had looked about him and said, I pick out that drab tortured girl to be interested in. I like the drab tortured one. She's the one I will stretch out my hand to.

February 12, 2021

Judge DeBose's courtroom today was incredibly composed and dramatic. You could hear a pin drop. It's not only that he keeps order but that people are spellbound by being in the presence of greatness. The docket was short and the proceedings were delayed because, being Mardi Gras time, all the police were out on the streets, so they couldn't testify.

He was briefly expounding on football during one of the many delays. "We're the Saints. We show up. Because we're professionals. But then we can't even beat the Giants." He went on in that vein for a while. Which was endearing in view of his meticulous judicial comportment.

At the end of the docket he always asks me if I have any questions (and I have a giant crush on him), so after the usual tedious inquiries about continuances, I asked him if the Saints were doing any better, since I like hearing him complain about them in that tortured way he has, alternating accolades with condemnation.

Next week all the courts are closed for Mardi Gras—with thirty murder cases pending on the docket.

February 16, 2021

My nerves were shot. It was Carnival. That meant I had to get up at six a.m. and dress up as a gigantic dice.

Forty years ago that's what it meant. Now it means I just lie low.

March 8, 2021

You don't always get to hear the real story in court because of all the boilerplate legal protocol, where the judge has to say the same lines over and over as if staging a play, and the huge random recesses where nothing happens, like on a movie set. Which makes the law boring at times. It reminds me of when people expect you to observe their religious rituals. How they're trying to make you fit in their mold.

The law is like pouring batter into a mold. A mold that it does not necessarily fit. But they have to pour the batter into the legal mold, because everything must be kept within the narrow parameters of legal procedure—what you can say, what you can't say. The law is a rigid mistress. You have to fit into its mold. And even if you don't fit, they have to stuff you into it. Like people who assume that you will observe their religious rituals.

I've done the same job in Maryland. The same job in Maryland is endlessly different from the one in New Orleans. In Maryland you have to have a partner every day in court and then confabulate with a bunch of ladies when you're filling out the forms. Because they don't trust you to do it all correctly on your own, and there is more likelihood of accuracy with a consensus. Which is actually a wise move, but in New Orleans you're strictly a lone wolf.

My preferred status.

The courthouse in Maryland was filled with giant signs that said DO NOT BRING EXPLOSIVES IN HERE. (OK, I'll just bring my explosives somewhere else?) After a string of shockingly paltry cases in civil court—a man complained that his neighbor poured glue on his car, a woman complained that a man in her office pushed her aside at the microwave—Tom and I went outside to discuss the cases and the paperwork. He was a fellow court watcher, a nice young man.

"There's something I have to tell you," said Tom after we had filled out the forms. "It's very serious." Gee, this is finally getting interesting, I thought. We're finally getting some drama around this place. I had never met him before that day. Then he dropped the bombshell: He was being dismissed. Canned. Fired. From a volunteer job.

He was very discreet when I asked him what the heck happened so I don't really know anything. I think I could have wormed it out of him but it seemed better to keep it fairly brisk. He mentioned something about lacking humility by having reported the incompetence of his fellow court watchers. At that point I loosened my collar and broke out into a slight sweat, since I'm obviously the most incompetent of them all.

In Maryland you're not allowed to read—the newspaper, a book—in court, despite the many interstices of time when nothing happens because of unexplained delays, recesses or bench conferences, etc. Whereas in New Orleans you can do whatever you want.

The thing that stays the same in New Orleans, defining a failed rotation (Kierkegaard's fear that things will NOT change), is the horrendous poverty of a kind you will not see anywhere else, adjacent to grandiose prosperity. "Downtrodden in many areas," I could say—but we all know what that means. It means unimaginable poverty. Anyone subjected to those conditions for centuries would go berserk. It's almost as if a scientific experiment in noble behavior is being conducted. How much can one group of people take and not go berserk? It irks me to observe the prosperous wondering why there is so much crime, as if unable to execute a math equation. But I don't exonerate myself for standing by while all this is going on.

March 15, 2021

I collated my records and identified the sources of my remorse:

Failure to act
Inability to be decorous/gracious/kind (snapped at guests)
Obsession with criticizing in-laws and their religious practices
Heartlessness and failure to empathize
Self-absorption
Being a bore
Self-congratulation/self-justification
Laziness/apathy/lack of energy
Spiritual paralysis
Overall impotence

Pretty succinct, I must say.

July 5, 2021

While looking for my missing treatise on *Don Giovanni* I read some old notebooks in New Orleans from my early twenties that were in my father's house in my old room. I found the person/girl who wrote them to be shockingly unpleasant and ridiculous and unworthy and lame. Other times I saw her quiet unsung deeds. And my heart bled for her. But if you want glory,

I guess go do something public and stop being so saintly and soft-spoken about it.

I stopped in the back patio of a café and sat on a couch under a ceiling fan where I read about ego disorders because I have one and I want to get to the bottom of it. Probably there is some kind of unsung hero thing of being ignored in my Freudian childhood script. Boys in the family were favored over girls in the South. The emotional response to this age-old lament is quite violent, though somehow more obscure when I'm up North.

Here it resonates with the clarity of a tuning fork.

July 6, 2021

Time went on. It was hurricane season. Malaise/damage from a year ago was still apparent on front porches packed with random stuff, masses of Mardi Gras beads choking the fences, defunct appliances thrown out on the curb awaiting nonexistent trash pickup. The tropical conditions and lack of prosperity were not conducive to efficient recovery.

A disturbing day in Judge Hollingsworth's courtroom, with fifty-nine items on the docket. During the course of the morning a defendant exposed himself on Zoom in his car while we were waiting for all the cases to be called. I wondered whether to report this shocking incident to my supervisor. Instead I recorded it in the comments section of the data-entry form. But who knows whether anyone reads my comments, which tend to be rather elaborate, on the data-entry form.

It was a prurient episode transporting me in a Proustian flashback to the time a guy exposed himself on the playground in front of my grandmother's house in childhood. As if it were all part of the local color—New Orleans—or key to the initial mysteries of life. In my report I seemed to be madly defending the guy who exposed himself, for some reason. Adelaide (my millennial daughter) says it's because I have Stockholm syndrome for the patriarchy.

July 7, 2021

Adelaide was in town working at an anarchist bookstore. We met for coffee after work. I had spent most of the day in Judge Blanchard's courtroom. Judge Blanchard was associated with vastly lowering the bail bonds of gang members, which would make Adelaide proud but many others worried.

Things sometimes got dicey when Adelaide's inability to modulate her crusade against injustice in a social setting clashed with certain members of the establishment—such as my stepmother—and I had to mediate or gloss things over.

Adelaide says I have Stockholm syndrome for my stepmother.

Then she rushed off to a leftist picnic.

*

I was staying at my childhood home.

"I don't have any diseases, but I'm obviously sinking," said my father, unraveling his cigars. He had taken to unraveling his cigars instead of smoking them.

We looked out at the teeming garden and the leaning palms. The paths were laid in sand and bordered by black pansies, amid the overgrowth in the sweltering heat. I questioned why he was unraveling the cigars, while dimly concluding that his constitution could no longer tolerate smoking five cigars per night.

"They're going to unravel eventually one way or another so I'm trying to beat them to the punch."

Seems like a metaphor for a lot of things.

Then I had to bid him adieu and go back to my regular life in the capital.

July 27, 2021

The lockdown isn't a problem for me as I'm pretty much always in lockdown. The virtual format persists, so I still get to monitor the courts in New Orleans even when I'm not there. And I'm not there a lot. Because I don't live there now.

And feel remorse to have forsaken it, and whenever I return, for the stark reality there is a constant rebuke.

Back in the courtroom of the heroic Judge Hollingsworth, who had seventy-eight items on her docket. A defendant on Zoom from the jail wanted to talk to her. His public defender wasn't there and Judge Hollingsworth is a stickler about that and won't talk to defendants without their lawyers in case they say something incriminating. But the defendant would not be silenced. He said he had been in jail for twenty-eight months and had missed Mardi Gras twice. It was determined that this is because his lunacy hearing keeps being postponed amid COVID and hurricane confusion.

The whole day was basically devoted to resetting matters due to hurricane-related damages/delays affecting everyone—of whose fortitude I am in awe. Their mode is often levity. Aside from the few who find Mardi Gras annoying, no one would let a little adversity get in the way of the revels. Such celebration is built into the personality of the town and by consequence the nature of the inhabitants.

So the curtain quaintly rises. The tragedies begin.

Intermission

My mother, trained as a psychologist, always thought that peoples' marriages were disintegrating and was always predicting disasters. Her predictions were always accurate. She knew the worst was coming. It would never surprise her. I always thought when she kept saying everything was disintegrating, that it wasn't really. But of course it turns out that it is. Unraveling, like my father's cigars.

A Yankee girl with high ideals transposed to New Orleans, she had to adjust to many alien dictates of the society surrounding her. Such as hosting an unnatural amount of parties.

"How was your dinner party?" I would ask her.

"It was harrowing."

"Harrowing?"

The frenetic pace of my mother's dinner parties is what is harrowing to contemplate. She was taught not only to give elaborate dinner parties, but their menus and seating arrangements she must record in a special leather-bound book so as not to embarrassingly repeat them for the same group. Everything about my mother seemed at odds with her fierce dedication to mastering these rituals. But she dutifully filled out all the categories—the details diagrammed like strategic battle plans—concluding with General Remarks, where she would summarize the outcome:

"Food extraordinarily good. Conversation extraordinarily excruciating."

And when it came to me—and/or the wastrel cohorts of my youth—she was one lone heroic soul who kept saying Pull yourself together, This is unacceptable.

If she saw a neurosis coming, she would draw her sword and prepare for battle.

I found the dinner-party books—the ones with all the seating arrangements and decorum—when I went through her effects. At first I marveled that she would so totally submit to the dictates of the society surrounding her. But it was the 1950s and she did what was expected of her. I would have swept it all aside, like a person clearing off her desk, in a vast Germanic rage. And I'm not 100 percent sure my mother had the faith in me that I have in my daughters; but maybe I am wrong.

She didn't pull any punches. She was strict, formidable, fierce. There must be discipline and there must be discretion—or there would be withering criticism.

Her withering criticism was not restricted by race, creed, or blood; it was distributed equally among all. Perhaps the most withering was reserved for anyone who ardently loved her. Perhaps to those she felt most bound to bestow the truth.

So I developed a spine. Nothing they can do can ever break me; though this is both good and bad. And since she died I wonder: who the hell now is going to bestow the truth?

I guess it's up to me.

Extraordinary Measures

"How is she?" asked Amelia on the telephone when I got to my father's house.

"She's gone," I said.

I had been summoned home to see my mother in the hospital when the end was near, but had not made it there before she died. My father met me at the airport gate. We embraced in tears when I stepped off the plane. I felt his heart beat racking in its fragile cage.

The funeral was planned.

"Do you want to see her?" asked the family friend who had taken charge of the arrangements.

"No, they don't want to see her," said my father. "It's not what she would have wanted."

My brothers and I did not dispute this firm decree. Cowed by the gravity of the occasion and by our father's grief. Also by Curry Carter, the family friend, who was stationed at a table in the living room making notes.

I was cowed by Curry Carter because he had always seemed to me to occupy a place at the pinnacle of high society, and

I felt that I did not fit in to high society. My father would have argued that in America there's no such thing as high society. But New Orleans had its own elaborate version of it, purportedly intended to be tongue-in-cheek, but not really succeeding in being tongue-in-cheek. Curry Carter was the arbiter of it. The kings and dukes of Carnival always stopped to toast him at his house on the parade route, where he served duck sandwiches and champagne.

It was odd that he and my father were such close friends. My father with his sober and pedantic bent, Curry Carter devoted to frivolity. But they had traversed the same green oak-lined streets together since they were boys, and this transcended the divergence of their ways.

My mother had been frail, but she had always been frail. A childhood affliction, polio, left her with some disabilities; but they did not disable her ability to be a bombshell. Her personality was so fierce, her gallantry so ingrained, that her death came as some surprise to us—though on a plane of rationality it was not surprising.

Curry Carter went on to make various decisions about the funeral.

A few days passed in a blur.

Amelia called again the night before the funeral.

"I wanted to tell you, Del, that I'm getting divorced," she said.

It was an odd time for her to be delivering this news.

*

Ten months later I was looking at the green Atlantic, amid the crashing elements, thinking of my mother, her atomic particles somewhere in the air. When I saw my father walking up—khakis, white bucks, the ancient blue sport jacket I knew so well—it was to see the missing other half.

"I was just thinking of you," I said.

"Del, I have something to tell you," he said. "You must have surmised by now."

He shed a tear. I held on tightly to him, looking at the vast Atlantic crashing. We both shed tears, and again I felt his heart beat wildly in its fragile cage.

"It might have been less hard for you if it had not been someone you were so close to."

We shed some more tears and I held on more tightly still.

The wedding would be in June. We stood on the crashing Atlantic in the night.

"I don't want to walk to the end of the horizon alone," he said.

I knew he needed someone to take care of him and travel with him. I knew Amelia's love for him was genuine. I ought not to repine. I could have stood at the crashing Atlantic longer with him but he said he was cold. We went inside.

He asked me to come back to his room and call her. At first I balked, saying it might take a day to frame my thoughts. But it was my duty. So he put her on the phone and I congratulated her. A gigantic electrical storm had suddenly developed. "And I hope you'll be a good mother to me," I kidded.

"Yes, don't stay out too late," she kidded back.

It's pretty hard to build a segue from being someone's dear friend to marrying their father, surely. She insinuated herself aggressively into all our hearts—that is not a crime.

Amelia had a gigantic crush on my father since the day I introduced them at a party ten years earlier and had pursued his friendship since that time, a weird and annoying fact. I had even mentioned it to my mother once. "This friendship between Amelia and my father seems a little annoying," I had said. My mother lay on her sickbed and made no comment. She looked away.

My father said Amelia had some furniture she wanted to bring in to the house.

"Some things are probably a bit threadbare around there," I agreed.

"When Gran painted my mother's room blue, it was a blow," he said, referring to his stepmother.

That was on the bottom rung of my emotional issues.

I wondered could I have been something less to Amelia than I had thought. Was it only my lack of generosity that prevented simple pure acceptance? Moving on from the daughter to the father. Greener pastures. She thinks it's OK to be your best friend and at the same time be your father's best friend. Is that weird?

Partly you feel duped.

The reality is more positive—she loves him, he loves her, she would enhance and prolong his life, she would look after him, we wouldn't have to. Magnanimity has its advantages.

When the newlyweds left the house for Paris and Amelia said her goodbyes, I bid her bon voyage. She put her hand on one side of my face and looked at me with an expression that was wistful, slightly sad, perhaps sorry she had caused me pain, or sorry that I hadn't understood. For me there was that element, however slight, of betrayal in it. The expression of a gruff, somewhat cynical worldly wisdom was in her face. Suave? Maybe. Jaunty? Not exactly, because there was more sorrow in it than that; maybe it was more like: Farewell friend—since I can't be the same friend when she's married to my father.

"How will she feel when he gets old and she has to take care of him?" my mother-in-law asked. My father, August Anhalt, was seventy-five and Amelia was forty-eight.

"She will consider it the honor and the purpose of her life," I said, which proved to be completely accurate.

That was the kind of love Amelia had for him, a fierce and reverent love. Was it a Catholic thing, of saintly duty? Maybe, but it was also a thing of: I cling to thee.

"If you can keep a man going past the age of seventy-five," said Amelia, "you can keep him going indefinitely."

This too proved to be completely accurate.

My friends growing up in New Orleans were all Catholic girls, and I often wondered about their Catholic qualities. They seem to have less vinegar in their veins than Jewish girls (like me). The Catholic girls came from wild alcoholic families and in my father's calm book-lined house they found an anchor in a storm. Amelia clung to it for dear life.

The magnolia tree outside of my old bedroom was dying, I discovered, after they were married. It languished in that state for ten years. Until the last vestiges of my resentment of Amelia were vanquished by the spectacle of her saintliness and devotion, her vast need of him; and then the dying magnolia was finally dead—like my resentment.

I was grateful when the languishing magnolia finally died, and my resentment with it. But from time to time it came back, like some rabid bamboo that overtakes your yard.

"Things ain't like they used to be, Mr. Anhalt," said the housekeeper after my mother died and the house and gardens were in disarray. But disintegration and decay had set in long before, near the end of my mother's life, when her domestic arrangements started to lose their spit and polish. Old bottles of Coke moldering in the side garden. It was definitely like a Gothic novel over there. So Amelia fit right in when she came, for Amelia had the air of someone standing at the edge of an abyss over a vortex of catastrophe, waiting for the worst, as if she had seen the worst before, as if possessed of the most tragic knowledge that could be known. In the Southern town that she had never left, she had seen it all. She had never been anywhere, but she had seen it all. It does take kind of a genius to do that.

It would seem at odds with this quality, but she was also terrified of everything—crossing the street, driving at night, mostly crime. She was always telling me stories about crime in the city with her atmosphere of pathological anxiety, and giving me articles about it from the newspaper. She constantly sent articles about diseases and crime sprees to her own daughters, unwittingly exacerbating their already rampant anxiety.

She was scared of everything—except her duty.

She was a strict creature. She whipped you into shape—as she must have done her daughters, as she did me when I became her stepdaughter. Yes she must have treated me as a stepdaughter then and not a friend. For I see how she whipped me into shape, in ways my mother never did. Her rules were:

OK, so you're visiting? Here is what's expected of you. Polite socializing with us is OK, within reasonable limits. Otherwise be helpful and stay out of the way.

It may sound harsh but in actuality describes the perfect houseguest. I can only dream of my own houseguests behaving that way.

She blindly honored my father's habits. The change into the ancient trousers from World War II after dinner, with the tray of seven cigars, the unnecessary butler... For me it was like a stage set there. Yet she took it seriously and blindly honored his ridiculous peccadilloes.

Handwritten notes were posted by Amelia throughout the house at strategic intervals, delivering instructions. Do not open this sliding glass door; it will become detached from its track. Do not attempt to open this cabinet; it is stuck. The ice maker is broken; do not seek ice. Confine shower to ten minutes; otherwise leaks.

The overall vibe was that of someone who does not wish to verbally or personally interact with visitors. Or of someone who does not engage in direct confrontation with them. And although Amelia studiously avoided direct confrontation, from her essence came an intense inner fierceness which emanated decision.

My mother had been a force to be reckoned with. My stepmother was a force that could not be reckoned with.

After Katrina society was still seen at parties along the Avenue uptown. Curry Carter in a wheelchair with an oxygen tank still attended every ball, still was toasted by the kings and dukes, stationed at his house on the parade route. The show must go on, was his attitude. To him it was a civic duty.

It was seventy degrees in the heart of winter, along the green dilapidated streets. There were parties everywhere. White awnings stretched from the porches to the sidewalks of houses uptown for weddings and receptions.

At the country club a series of white tents had been put up over the tennis courts. Men in white-tie and tails with blue ribbons across their chests and dowagers in ball gowns doddered through the Grill. They were having a series of balls in the tents after dinner.

"Run-down balls," according to my father. Mardi Gras balls relocated to the tennis courts after their normal venue was damaged in the hurricane.

My father's life had been defined by hurricanes and floods since 1927. Thus he had hurricane fatigue and had stayed through the storm. When we finally planned his rescue—for he was eighty at the time—he was focused on somehow getting enough cigars to last for the duration of his absence. If you're ever swept away by a cataclysm, bring your cigars.

Things were different since Katrina. The scrappy quality. The gentility still there but its veneer chipped. Its shabbiness increased. Its uncertainty. Rather than being cloaked so heavily in its former certainties.

A well-dressed elderly woman walking by amid the run-down ball-goers made some remarks to Amelia.

"Who was that?" I asked when she ambled off.

"That's Shorty Van Horn. She has no idea who or where she is."

Being elderly, most of my father's friends had diseases or were in tragic declines. There was the decline but not the fall.

Jiggy Delancey staggering past, encased in white-tie and tails.

"What is Jiggy a nickname for?" I asked.

"It's short for a jigger of booze," said Amelia.

The crowd in the Grill had thinned out when we finished dinner, but the run-down ball was hopping. Society men dressed as harlequins and dukes were weaving out under the awnings, the plumes of their ridiculous satin fezzes rising toward the oaks. "What kind of man," I mused, "would want to dress up like a harlequin in a mask and parade around like that in public places? He would have to be a drinker," I deduced.

"New Orleans is a society of drunks," pronounced Amelia.

The chimes of the cathedral rang out, as in all old Catholic cities. That was somehow part of it. The Catholics drank. They tended to drink.

Whereas my father, August Anhalt, had a stern Germanic backbone and his mind was like a Germanic steel trap. He had kept a record of every book he'd read since 1950. He showed it to me when we got home. At the moment he was reading an eight-hundred-page book called *Pseudodoxia Epidemica*, which was apparently a barrel of laughs, because he kept chuckling at his desk when he read it after dinner with his cigars.

The temperature in my father's house was freezing. For a man who lived his entire life in a tropical climate, he had a dramatic phobia of hot weather. When he was a boy and air-conditioning was not yet in wide use, he slept on the porch in summer. He lived in the house he was born in.

I sometimes wondered why it didn't suffocate him. To live in the house you were born in. Largely it was a matter of practicality. Still, it's the mystery of one's father.

It was different for me. I knew this town and I were meant to part. That formed the basis of my nostalgia for it.

Twenty years passed. Amelia's love for my father was more than genuine. It was a love so fierce that I have rarely, if ever, seen its like. Her love for my father might more accurately be described as adoration, and she served his needs in a saintly and somewhat outmoded manner that came to be inspiring.

Now there was the spectacle of the valiant nonagenarian whose life had always been run with Germanic precision and mental acuity, and the pathologically anxious younger woman who adored him and devoted herself to him. It was a spectacle to fill one with compassion. She had given him the will to live for years beyond the allotted time.

Whenever I flew in, a terrible storm would start about forty-five minutes before landing. You practically had to defy death to go there. Everything was black, or gray; occasionally you would see a glimpse of the Mississippi River glittering under the black storm clouds.

The first thing we learned in grade school, for some reason—and we learned it over and over—was how to spell Mississippi. I tried to focus on that to distract myself from the horrible lurches of the plane through the storm, the view obscured by blackness, except when illuminated by a flash of lightening.

When we were about to descend, the pilot suddenly brought the plane back up, being unable to land in the violent conditions. He held above the clouds for a while until trying to land again, going through the same thing several times. Everyone was completely silent and dignified. I saw an actual tornado hit the runway on one of the pilot's daredevil attempts to descend. Finally he made the landing.

My father gave me some Homer to read to calm me down when I got home. I thought of my mother: it was her birthday. Here is the mysterious source, of why I am meek, because she was so fierce.

I mentioned the birthday to my father. He said he was well aware of the day.

"In many respects she was a wonderful person," he said.

Gee, could you be any less qualified or enthusiastic, I mean, this is the woman you were married to for forty years.

"But you know my story."

It was endlessly curious that it was now my story also, though I did not confide the truth to my father. Usually a girl becomes her mother. I became my father—the sternness, the innocence, the shock.

The Anhalts stayed together. August Anhalt wanted to live with his children. We were still young when it happened. I was a child. In his day the mother would be granted full custody no matter the circumstances.

But he never forgave her; and this was something I could never understand. He didn't forgive. Or did he? He said he didn't. But they lived together for the next forty years, until he took her through the door to heaven, steadfast to the end, as she must have known he would be.

It was written on stone, palm fronds, and the hearts of men. He too was very gallant.

After dinner we sat in the library, my father unraveling his cigars. Behind the house the gardens sweltered in the heat.

"So sorry about Curry Carter," I said to my father.

"Thank you."

"When is the funeral?"

"He's not dead yet."

"Oh. How is he?" I asked.

"You mean does he still have joie de vivre? Yes."

"And how is Amelia?" I asked.

"She's looking at a long widowhood so she's anxious."

"Gee, could you be any more blunt and direct?"

He was glued to his desk as usual in the evening after dinner. Studying ancient Greek, digitizing his files, and disencumbering himself of his twenty-two trusteeships in view of retirement.

Also he was writing an alphabetized index or catalog of what he likes, with photographs and text. For example under *P*: Palladian Villas to Peat Stacks. Like who ever heard of a peat stack.

"Do you think an artist has to be crazy?" I asked him.

"Couldn't hurt," he said crisply, unraveling his cigars.

A marching band came out of nowhere and could be heard on Webster Street. I ran outside to look and saw it turn down Constance heading for the park. Mardi Gras rehearsals: drumbeats in the distance, impending gaiety—like the parades that came down Dominican Street in the Black Pearl when I was little. I would walk to the church on the corner with Franciola, who would be singing the latest soul songs; I was wearing a pair of Mardi Gras beads that I exulted in, and as we approached the Avenue, the world was wide with hope. But a shimmering realm of promise led beyond it to the outer world.

2.

It was some months after my father started unraveling the cigars that I was home again. In the middle of the night while getting out of bed he collapsed and lay semiconscious on the floor. Amelia came upstairs and got me but we could not bear his weight to get him back in bed. The ambulance was called. The emergency medical technicians did various tests to evaluate the patient before taking him to the hospital.

"If the unthinkable happens do you want us to use extraordinary measures?" they asked.

"As extraordinary as possible," said Amelia. "Give it everything you've got."

Extraordinary measures were taken. Like Dostoyevsky at the firing line, he prepared to face death and then got a reprieve. He was in the hospital for three months. He was not himself.

Adelaide was in town working at the anarchist bookstore. She and I visited my father every evening in the hospital. Visiting hours were from five to eight p.m. Before we left the first day we showed him how to use the call button if he needed the nurse.

"And what do I say if she comes?" he asked.

"You tell her what you need," said Adelaide.

"So if she comes, I express my needs."

"Exactly."

I was at the hospital every evening from five until eight, to take over for Amelia who did not like to drive at night. I did treasure that time with my father, and thought I performed an important service during those hours, though after all what I did could be done by others, so really it was more for me.

The nurse came in and asked about the do-not-resuscitate forms. Amelia was in charge of that. Later the nurse returned and asked us if we wanted to take Communion. If we wanted the doddering Catholic priest to come by to give us Communion. First she asked him his religious affiliation. He said Jewish.

Then she asked us if we wanted to take Communion. After a perplexed silence, I said I wouldn't mind, but it might be sacrilegious.

Later I asked if he would like to hear some opera, which I played for him on my device. It was he who had inspired my love of opera by bravely taking me to Salzburg when I was a stoned-out teenager who everyone found annoying. He sang a bit of one aria; he smiled during another. *The Abduction from the Seraglio*, *The Marriage of Figaro*, and *Don Giovanni*.

When the night nurse got there at eight o'clock to take over I said to my father, "Remember Quandra?"

"Who could forget Quandra?" he said in a quiet voice.

The next day he started having delusions. Mainly his delusions revolved around Switzerland. He also asked me if my husband Jack was involved with the Russians and calmly indicated that he thought Jack was working undercover. Hostile government forces, etc.

Later Stokes came in. He was the night sitter. During the day he worked in the psychiatric ward, which was on that same floor. He had to hold people down when they tried to escape or commit suicide, he said.

We lost the Saints game. Stokes said it was rigged. He had an extremely heavy Mississippi accent. My father loves him. Says Stokes knows a lot about the world.

Any mention of Switzerland? asked Amelia when I got

home. She was eating a tragic salad alone in the dining room where they had always dined together, the table elaborately set. I do think that by sheer force of her resolve Amelia will get him going. She had always kept him going before.

The hospital was depressing sometimes. There was a retired judge who never figured out his call button so he just lay there calling Help Help.

"At least he doesn't play the violin anymore," said someone.

"He played the violin?"

"He was terrible."

Amelia told me to park in the garage because it was connected by an indoor pedestrian bridge to the hospital, but it was a maze over there that I was always getting trapped in. I preferred to park on the street, a prospect which filled her eyes with abject terror. She kept sending me videos and articles about violent crime and carjackings.

"The anxiety within is greater than the circumstances outside—of my soul or my control—so it doesn't make me nervous," I said. My comment was intended to offer another perspective that might quell her anxiety.

But what makes me think I should go around advising people of my wisdom all the time? Seems kind of obnoxious.

"I have a nameless melancholy," said Adelaide.

"Is it because of your grandfather so weak in the hospital?" I asked.

"Well no, I think it's because this guy I liked ghosted me."

A house was burning on the Avenue. The Avenue was closed to traffic, blocked off, swarming with tourists and bystanders watching the fire. Someone sent me a note to say it was the Curry Carter house. The one with all the parties at the pinnacle of high society, where the dukes and kings of Carnival stopped to toast the occupants. The family vowed to rebuild and to still toast the king of Rex from the site, be it from lawn chairs in front of the ruins. I marveled that the burning of this house was front-page news here, above the fold, as it duly ran the next day in that format.

Amelia asked that we shield the patient from this news.

A nurse came in to do the feeding tube, which was one of the extraordinary measures. He asked her if he would still need it when he went home. The nurse kind of went into a long hemming and hawing and I couldn't tell if it reflected a refusal to speak the truth or genuine confusion or general policy; but my father is a man of truth, I felt sure. He knew how to cross-examine a witness and he wasn't getting answers.

"Dad, you know I'm a straight shooter, right?"

"Yes, I raised you that way."

"I think it's basically permanent. Also it's a way to get your meds."

"OK."

The nurse went on to tell us that one lady made her put martinis in her feeding tube.

As the evening wore on he wanted to be turned to his other side. We talked about how to do it and analyzed the bed and I asked if I should try to turn him and he said No we'd better wait for Quandra.

"You're heroic, Del," he added, doubtless to be kind.

"Not heroic enough to turn you over, though," I said.

A disease contracted in New Guinea, where he worked in intelligence and code-breaking in World War II, bulbar polio, had somehow returned, which prevented him from swallowing and caused bits of food or tobacco to aspirate directly into his lungs. He had been sinking because he could not really eat. The doctor said a permanent feeding tube was the only solution. Upon first hearing this when he arrived at the hospital, my father said No, I've had a long life.

That was the fork in the road.

Help, help! called the retired judge, who couldn't find his call button, as I went down the hall.

The Curry Carter house burned to the ground. My father knew about it. He seemed to take it in stride—this final conflagration of Curry Carter's earthly significance. His earthly existence had also by then concluded.

Across the Avenue from his house was the Intangibles Club with its faded green awnings, where he went most nights to meet with his cronies. He had developed the purplish look of the hopeless alcoholic. His drinking got out of hand, and one night he collapsed at the club. The old gents summoned Sylvester, his attendant, who helped him into the car and drove him to the hospital. There, due to a mixture of alcohol poisoning and diabetes, the doctors amputated his legs after diagnosing a heart attack brought on by poor circulation. He lived, but he languished in the hospital for seven months. At first his vitality failed to return. He seemed stunned. Yet once he became accustomed to the situation, the life returned to his spirit. Even a speck of gaiety lit his heart. It was thus that without his legs, in his wheelchair, decimated and reduced like the city itself, he went on to give the best parties and throw black-tie events, greeting his guests at the door in his wheelchair, with Sylvester standing behind gripping the handles.

His basic reaction to the catastrophic course of events was to give more parties. Like Wellington and his troops attending a ball in Brussels the night before Waterloo to psych out the enemy.

I don't know who the enemy was for Curry Carter, as it seemed not only death that he meant to defy. He died the day after his hundredth birthday party, an event he felt obligated to attend.

After the ball is over I'll die.

At his funeral I saw one of his daughters turn in her seat to give someone a look of jazzy complicity that seemed to telegraph the message: We're jazzy, even at a funeral, we need alcohol, soon we'll be able to get some. Melancholy is not an emotion that type of person felt comfortable with presenting to the world. All of his daughters were like that. Curry Carter was like that too. My father was never really their type of person, but they were dear to him.

In the hospital people watch a lot of TV. The TV always seemed to be on in the background with its hectoring inanities. There were some hectoring forensic crime shows my father seemed bewitched by. He had never been one to watch TV before in his life. Too busy reading *Pseudodoxia Epidemica*, etc.

At home Amelia asked me how I thought he was. She was worried about the cigars. Will he try to keep smoking them, will he somehow get his hands on them—when they were a source of his collapse: the aspirated particles of tobacco.

How was he going to get these cigars? I suggested. He could not move without assistance, and I don't think anyone would accede to a request to get him a cigar. I'm probably the only sapsucker who would, but even I wouldn't. Too scary. All you need is a brain to understand.

I wished I could assuage her anxieties. I wished I could

advise her: This great love you've had, it is not given to many. Be grateful for it. Maybe it becomes an abstraction, an ideal, but therefore it will endure.

That is probably not helpful to someone focused on the here and now. Even before my father's collapse she told me she had seen Margaret Stone, a recent widow, in the grocery store, and Margaret Stone was smiling. How could she be smiling, Amelia wanted to know. How could she go on.

To me the answer was clear. During the Battle of Waterloo one of Wellington's generals looked down and said in surprise to the duke, "By God, I've lost my leg." Wellington looked at it and confirmed crisply, "By God, so you have." And then they went on with the battle. Talk about an iron nerve. By George, some things are difficult. Let's get on with it.

You have to have an iron nerve.

But I am a heartless maniac, blithe and cold. What planet are you from, lady? I keep asking myself. What planet am I living on, to be so coldhearted? I don't know.

One of my former students—now a fifty-five-year-old white-haired man from Virginia who mysteriously was able to quit his job six years earlier to devote himself to writing a seven-hundred-page sweeping saga of the Arctic in Olde English that I had to tactfully suggest to him might be boring—was always asking me: Is that really the message you want to leave your children with? Let's get on with it?

Yes. Don't fall apart. Meet what comes—with strength. Sangfroid. Courage.

I wished I could convey to Amelia that she could do this.

Or is the only way to suffer less by loving less?

Anhedonia

After a few months the situation with my father stabilized and he was home, surrounded by adoring women—his wife and an array of rotating nurses. He was rickety but suave—like New Orleans.

Spring came suddenly to the capital, a brief but towering spring. Followed by a swamp-laden, allergy-ridden summer.

I had been relegated to accommodate a beach house for a swarm of houseguests mainly consisting of my husband's relatives. Which was annoying, kind of in the same way that being expected to fulfill the dictates of my mother's dinner-party books would have annoyed me. But it is a universal truth of life that many people and things are annoying, and that finding an effective way to deal with this is important.

The first basic thing is to identify and quantify what is annoying and why. The next thing is to move forward, noting that annoyance is unavoidable and inevitable in life. Rather than kind of sinking further into paralysis and rage at each annoyance.

Annoyance turns to wrath if you're not careful. Not that wrath is so bad. It's kind of a more stern form of annoyance. Maybe a more elevated form. I don't know. But I do know that if you let it get out of hand, pretty soon you're looking at the wrath of Achilles.

Some people respect people who never say anything bad about anyone. I'm not one of those people. I'm also not one of those people who never say anything bad about anyone.

Take my houseguests. My houseguests keep going berserk. It's like the wrath of Achilles—the wrath of my houseguests. The atmosphere is tense, houseguests breathing down your neck, feeling their wants and needs wafting through at all times. Like why can't houseguests try to be airy burdenless presences?

A lot of the criticism comes from my sister-in-law, Stella. I thought it was coming from everyone. Then I realized it emanates only from Stella, but is so intense that it seems like it's coming from all directions in a vast chorus. She thinks I don't like her. OK fine—is it not then an endeavor incumbent on you to behave likably? Of course that's funny coming from me. Why am I such a dick, is the big question.

Ordinarily no one pays me any mind whatsoever. I am ensconced in vast depths of solitude that no one else on the face of the earth would be able to tolerate. Maybe that's why.

A friend and neighbor effusively invited everyone to stay at her beach house on the July Fourth weekend. I assumed she had gone insane—because of the crowds in this location at that time. She wrote effusive notes to the upcoming houseguests about kayaking and food preferences. They all wrote effusive notes back about how much they love kayaking and what their food preferences are. Reading the thread I was just totally: Are you insane?

Why am I so crabby, you ask? That's the million-dollar question. Maybe because everyone is being so effusive. Plus it keeps escalating. They think everything is wonderful. Everything is not wonderful, obviously. In fact realizing that things are not wonderful is the key to life. Then you can go forward with your shoulders squared to meet what comes.

What came was the houseguests with their high hopes and breakfast preferences. It took some of them eleven hours to drive there from Washington on a Friday in summer, and their host expected them to drive back on Sunday. So with all the fruit choices and what kind of yogurt they like, there's actually a pretty tight rein on the largesse.

But why is my favorite subject how annoying some people are? Like the fire only burns when people are annoying me and when I marvel at their inability to—to what, be like me? Obviously I have an ego disorder.

Why am I such an obnoxious anhedonic misanthrope? Washington, DC, is probably an enhanced breeding ground for my anhedonia.

We moved to the capital shortly after 9/11. BOMB THREAT CAUSES MASS ENNUI ran the headline in the *Washington Post*. Actually that was pretty dashing. Sheer gallantry, really. I had gallantly moved to the capital to get bombed off the face of the earth, perhaps.

Washington is a government town, so everyone acts like federal tax bureaucrats, just by osmosis. You find yourself using words like "legislative bodies"—words you've never used before—at dinner parties. Driving in our neighborhood at certain hours involved a miasma of pointless rules and regulations prohibiting right turns so you had to take a crash course in geometry to figure out how to get to your house.

Before Washington we lived in California. In California you're driving along a freeway lined by massive boulders and bald hills and you think, Wow, this isn't very homey. Plus, why is it so big? Everything is huge—a highway, a canyon, a bald hill. But your human soul adjusts, and then you think: I possess these massive stark bald hills in my soul. I have bent them to my will—or they have bent mine to theirs.

There is always that defining moment when a place becomes home. Though as I can't really bend the legislative bodies to my will, I don't know if that defining moment will ever come in the capital.

I was in an extremely bad mood most of the time when the kids were growing up in Washington. I was always monitoring their requests to vet them for overkill. To see if when they asked me to jump, they were asking me to jump too high. I did not want to spoil them, after all.

Is that a crime? I think not.

Though if I were a healthier person I would play ping-pong and drink wine and cook dinner for ten people and be a happier healthier more hedonistic person who can go out and just live life.

It's a problem.

One key to it all is realizing how annoying you yourself are. Like how all my houseguests see me as a heartless maniac. The main issue yesterday was my unanswered prayers to help my personality. Ditto today.

Why is a person an empty vessel of insecurity—what is this vagary, why does the ego need nonstop confirmation to restore its fragile balance. We must quantify these ills to make them go away:

Insecurity. Ego Problems. Anhedonia. Operatic Wrath.

These are the lions at the gate—the point is to banish them.

Some people have operatic angst at the minor annoyances of life. This is wrong—misplaced wrath. The point is you want to calm down. You want to make your peace with things. Because you don't want to go through life seething with wrath.

Though it kind of seems like I'm the one seething with wrath.

The problem with my houseguests is that they're slobs. And my whole obsession is bringing order out of chaos.

Once I had the perfect houseguest. Every afternoon at five sharp he'd start mixing a gigantic pitcher of cocktails and reveal shocking secrets of his life, which was very diverting. He brought flowers, he brought groceries, he rescued a turtle that was being raped by another turtle. After a somewhat tense wait for dinner—which he alone cooked, with the same utter dedication as he applied to the giant pitcher of cocktails—he grilled the fish, he cooked, he cleaned, he did everything in a most exemplary manner, the best houseguest you could possibly imagine.

And yet, my in-laws found him objectionable. Typical.

In-laws are the source of an immense amount of wrath. I would also put certain attitudes toward religion in this category. Orthodoxy is not necessarily annoying in itself, but it is highly annoying if an orthodox person expects you to automatically embrace his customs or perform religious rituals with the same enthusiasm he does, as his enthusiasm is not contagious.

So it's a person pursuing his agenda and being super excited about it and expecting everyone else to be excited about it too.

Maybe that doesn't sound like a huge crime. Honestly it might be less offensive if the person's agenda was, let's say, basket weaving, something random and secular and unpolitical, but it's annoying because religion does have a sacred quality and can't really be forced.

I was thrilled to be back in New Orleans criminal court on the Zoom with Judge Hollingsworth. She's still mad as hell, and it is incredibly rejuvenating to see a black woman in New Orleans who everyone is quaking in fear of because she's tough and she's the one calling the shots.

She should be my role model with the houseguests. I considered Amelia's technique—the handwritten notices everywhere—but I didn't have Scotch tape and I don't fear direct confrontation. It was the aura of Amelia I was going for—squelching your spirit and inspiring fear.

Now I see Judge Hollingsworth might be an even better role model. Arms akimbo, "this is unacceptable," "this is embarrassing," "I'm going to take this to the media if it doesn't stop," everyone quaking in fear, snapping to, shaping up, etc.

You might be wondering where this beach house is that I keep talking about. My husband bought this beach house. I had nothing to do with it. I didn't want my anhedonia to squelch his dreams by trying to talk him out of it. It is in Long Island. I have hesitated to identify the location because of its obnoxious connotations. Talk about extremes—there's a lot of grandiosity around here, not in obvious contrast to abject poverty, but to regular people with modest accommodations, ours included, a house in the woods, and by the way, woods are scary. So it's not shocking and scandalous in the same way as the extreme disparities in New Orleans.

I don't know who the people are who live in the grandiose places. It's a thirty-minute drive from our house in the woods to the raging Atlantic Ocean, where the old mansions range among the marshes like a stage set.

If you scratch the surface of this place I'm sure you'd find that its real essence is in the raging ocean and the rugged rule of nature, including animals and bugs and woods, and other wild and scary things that humans have not truly encroached upon, believe it or not, as these things are closely guarded by the authorities here.

These things are not closely monitored in New Orleans. The infrastructure is crumbling: police quitting in droves, garbage collection at a standstill, the streets torn up with huge inexplicable potholes everywhere, and unfinished drainage-system drilling conducted by questionable Army Corps of Engineers and a purportedly corrupt levee board.

My kids grew up on a regular street in an American town—a suburban glen of the capital that looked like a Norman Rockwell poster. It had a lot of white-haired people who were amazingly cheerful on a frequent basis. What did they have to be so cheerful about? There were a lot of rules and regulations. That kept things viable. That kept them functional.

New Orleans was a place where your father lived in the house he was born in and was downtown all day with the cronies he had known since nursery school and whose fathers had known each other since ditto. Those were the rules. They ruled the roost. You would always see in some parts of town unimaginable squalor and decay and poverty unlike what you would see anywhere else, because you would never see anything that bad anywhere else.

Some devote their lives to understanding it. Some in my own family had. The naked bulb had always been too harsh for me. You did not look too closely, or looked the other way, or fled.

Observed via Zoom in the New Orleans criminal courtroom of Judge Anne Satterwhite (who is white). I was somewhat traumatized by her behavior. Her first trial since 2019 was scheduled (rape/murder, cruelty to juvenile) and she was super excited about it. A defense lawyer kept trying to obstruct it. One of the witnesses was dead, he said. Murdered. Another witness was confronted in the courtroom this morning by gang members and threatened.

"Child-rapist murderer," complained the defense lawyer, describing the witness.

"Sticks and stones," said the judge. "Name-calling."

"This witness would perjure himself," argued the defense lawyer.

"Everyone in my courtroom has lied to me," said the judge.

This defense lawyer was a little rude. Judge Satterwhite seemed to know him and did not take offense.

"Is everyone going to behave in this trial?" she asked.

"I'm not the one calling perjurers to the witness stand," said the defense lawyer.

"I love you, man," said the judge—when you'd think she'd cite him for contempt.

I haven't mentioned what the judge did that traumatized me. Which you can crystallize into two words by quoting the curse words she used (shit and fuck) during the proceedings. While delivering an existential monologue like a country-music singer having a nervous breakdown on the stage. When I filed my data I tactfully mentioned her meandering style instead of baldly reporting that she used curse words from the bench. Because I felt like a supercilious, sanctimonious snitch. But I can't think of another judge who would let that slip.

During the interstices I researched Judge Satterwhite and instantly came across various scandals she has been involved in from the bench, including a sexual-harassment suit filed against her by a clerk.

I attended a social event. The wedding of a friend of Adelaide's. Adelaide had to go somewhere with the bridesmaids first so it was just: Will I be able to cope socially? After being so much of a recluse. I mean a misanthrope. I would practice my social skills there.

A gorgeous winding drive led up a shining hill overlooking the ocean on a green lawn with tropical-cocktail-attired guests. I milled around for a while gawking at them. When the buffet line started I got in it. I can't hold my liquor so I was ready to eat. I sat down alone at a table and started eating dinner in my lonely splendor. Soon a young man sat down beside me. He had horn-rimmed glasses and brown hair in wings parted in the middle—he looked like the Great Gatsby. He also had my favorite body type in a man: portly. Thank the Lord, I thought, and started plying him with questions.

It turned out he worked on Capitol Hill. I plied him with questions about what it was like working for the lying sack of swizzle sticks (as the comments section of the *Washington Post* used to call him) who previously ran the place. The world's literally most obnoxious person. At the moment he was out of office but was always in the background, still haunting our national psyche and international reputation, planning his revenge and return. Here's something that he could never understand:

The best thing about the capital was the spirit of the man it had been named for. Every time they drew him to a post, he would agonize and ultimately accept, but always stand up and say: "I just want it on record that I do not consider myself equal to this task."

This was his basic position on everything. Showing that even the great have self-doubt. Maybe only the great.

I liked everything about him. His purported inability to tell a lie. His endearing penchant for self-effacement, his lack of being power-mad. The original ideals.

The long-haired romantic public defender in New Orleans told me he thinks everyone deserves (or is capable of?) redemption. Which he enacts while pursuing his vocation as a public defender. His unflinching ideals have stayed with me. Though I'm not sure I agree with them.

Some people are beyond redemption. The barnacles you can't scrape off the boat. Like this moronic maniac who is incapable of any comprehension of the word "ideals." He wouldn't know an ideal if he ate it every day for breakfast. He wouldn't understand the meaning of the word "remorse" if it were blazoned across the sky.

Don Giovanni keeps playing in my head, as if to drown him out.

The sun hung low in the west in a spectacular golden orb that shed its deeply golden light glinting over everything—very beautiful, but like in a disaster movie where actually the whole place is about to explode or aliens have landed in their glinting silver spaceship from Mars.

Judge Anne Satterwhite much more in control today. A whole different picture. Though at one point she was promoting Alcoholics Anonymous to an incarcerated defendant in such detail re: how it works, etc., that you definitely got the feeling she has been there. Ditto when discussing with a forensic psychologist whether an incarcerated defendant was taking his Adderall.

The forensic psychologist described himself as verbose. He apologized for his verbosity but he was actually quite succinct. The upshot was that he recommended the defendant incompetent to stand trial.

Judge Satterwhite was dubious. "He's accused of killing two people," she said. "And the previous psychologist said he was malingering." She went on to yell at various people including the clerk of court, the supervisor, and whoever had not served detectives meant to be testifying in court with notice to appear, causing the cases to be reset.

I haven't seen as much righteous wrath in this judge before. Usually she's in her life-of-the-party mode. Which is probably what detracts some credibility from the righteous wrath.

"Is everything wrong since Katrina? Or Ida? It's like everything is broken," she ruminated to the court at large. "Something's gotta make sense around here, y'all."

Such an odd mixture of astute plus I'm-at-a-Cocktail-Party. My take is when she tries to be tough, she kind of lacks the cred, because of the Southern belle at a cocktail party thing.

Unfortunately she reminds me of myself.

My doppelganger in this respect. Maybe that's why my houseguests don't take me seriously.

*

"What's Adelaide doing?" asked my father in New Orleans.

"She's working at an anarchist bookstore. Also she's writing a book."

"What is she writing a book about?"

"The patriarchy—how it must be torn down."

"Don't forget the matriarchy. That's very dangerous too."

"How's your book going?" I asked my daughter Adelaide.

"I'm either sitting at my computer sobbing or sitting five feet away from my computer looking at it sobbing."

Deadlines and nerves, I know, and the brilliant girl's self-doubt. But also the patriarchy. For me it was the way of the world. Whereas Adelaide seeks to change the world.

Judge Satterwhite was out today and a retired judge was standing in.

A proliferation of new scandals involving her have arisen. The sexual-harassment suit seems to be at the top of the list.

The next day Judge DeBose had to get through fifty items on the docket in three hours. Three court watchers were observing him for no reason. Actually the reason was that Judge Satterwhite was out again with no one standing in, and two other sections were closed, so they crammed all the court watchers into his courtroom.

She seems to be unraveling.

Returning to DC we went to the tennis tournament held in the swamp-laden depths of August there. The weather was cloudy. When dark fell, white bats flew on court once or twice.

Benoît Paire, a temperamental Frenchman who has tantrums on the court, jumping up and down on his racket trampling it to bits, was in a long slog with some boring guy from Slovenia. The problem is that this temperamental Frenchman doesn't really have what it takes. What it really takes is the simple but all-guiding desire to win. If you don't have that, forget it. Usually when watching a match you can always tell, one player is driven by this simple overweening idea: I WANT TO WIN. I WILL NEVER GIVE UP. The other, like the temperamental Frenchman, is not. His attitude is: I'm stuck in this grind, this rat race, and I have a talent, but I don't have this overweening desire to win; I'll put up a fight to the extent that I will lose a gruelingly close five-set match, which is incredibly hapless and pretty tragic. It makes you wonder why I'm still in this game, but this is how I earn my living.

At Wimbledon in his match against a short but determined Argentinian it was the exact same story. Benoît Paire duly embodied his profile of mental instability and perfected his ability to give up. He was given a violation for Not Trying. Everyone booed. He hurled his racket to the ground and jumped up and down on it in a rage. He lost the set 6-0—and the match in three sets.

Formerly my hero was Federer. When he lost a match late in his career I asked my father in New Orleans, "What exactly happened, do you think? I couldn't bear to watch it."

"An old fighter went into the ring once too often."

"I couldn't bear to look at his opponent whatsoever," I said. "He's probably the greatest jerk who ever lived."

"But a shark is always dangerous, even an old shark," said my father. "Think of the inscription at Thermopylae: O stranger, tell the Spartans that here we died fighting."

Judge Satterwhite announced her retirement. It was not too surprising. You could sort of tell her days were numbered. Kind of sad that the show is over. I mean, since she's nuts.

And the show *is* over, because so is the pandemic, and they're canceling the Zoom.

So what happened to the theme? The houseguests, the in-laws, the annoyances, etc. I kept getting more and more annoyed while writing about them until I became a simmering mass of unfocused rage. The desired result was not being achieved.

I know how to not have operatic wrath at the minor annoyances of life—the plumber doesn't come, it rains on your garden party, the chandelier falls out of the ceiling, your in-laws don't appreciate you.

But now you see it coming on again. The wrath. The anhedonia.

Maybe let's calm down about the anhedonia. I think it's a reaction to my wild youth in New Orleans. In my decadent youth I continually emerged unscathed from drunken boating accidents, boating accidents in hurricanes, or getting struck by lightning on the golf course in a hurricane. What were we doing on the golf course in a hurricane? Exactly. Not playing golf.

So now I take it to the opposite extreme. Something in Shakespeare made it clear. Like I'm probably the only person on the face of the earth who finds Falstaff (the ultimate hedonist) annoying. When with astonishing cruelty (according to the scholars) Henry V, in his sudden transformation from wayward wastrel youth to king, publicly humiliates Falstaff by delivering the completely unsurprising news that he and all his cronies will not get top positions or preferential treatment at the court.

I know thee not, old man. Presume not that I'm the thing I was. I'm not who I used to be.

2.

I read in the newspaper that New Orleans was badly flooded in a hard rain. I tried to call but could not reach the folks at home. Amelia was running a massive operation dependent on a chain of technical assistance (nurses, tubes) that if disrupted by hurricanes, Mardi Gras, etc., would have the most dire consequences. No wonder she met my father's trials with crippling anxiety, borne forward by her gigantic love. It was a spectacle for the ages, really. One person and her gigantic love got him going again and gave him the will to go on.

But it was a dire operation she was running and I worried about her.

"You are sublimating your concern for your father into this worry for Amelia," said Louise Brown.

Maybe so. But I wasn't sure. The wife hangs on for dear life. The daughter is able to let go. It sounds like I'm suggesting we smother the patient with a pillow. The wife conducts the long goodbye. Now it sounds like I'm trying to smother him with a pillow again. But I was kind of bitter about the extraordinary measures. Some people keel over one fine day in a swift and sudden death without suffering. My mother would have preferred the sudden keeling over to the long slow decline. Maybe most people would. Some people hang on until the other person can let them go.

Then he was back in the hospital with pneumonia. So I was on a plane for home. The usual mad careening through the storms while sending prayers to God—until you saw the Mississippi River snaking through the land, and the Black Pearl where I was born. You practically had to defy death to go there, careening through the storms.

You had to defy death to live there. You could blow it all over with a feather much less a hurricane. I always thought you'd have to be fairly madcap to live there.

"Tell me about the Mallorys," I said to my father in the hospital, to make conversation. They were his law partners.

"Monroe was hard, a hard father; so Phelps was an alcoholic. Monroe had nine siblings, just like my father."

"How did you handle it—when Phelps would stagger around drunk at the office—what did everyone say?"

"What could they say? He was the boss."

We discussed my obsession with Don Giovanni. I asked him who was the greatest Don Giovanni of all time.

Ezio Pinza, he said promptly. That night I found a recording of this production, staged in 1945, and its beauty is so thrilling that it makes even Erwin Schrott look slightly pale.

The next day we went on to have a rollicking conversation about it despite his being flat on his back in the hospital and overtly weak. I diverted him with Ezio Pinza, Erwin Schrott, and a comparison of their portrayals of Don Giovanni. I only played the briefest bit of the Ezio Pinza recording for him. I knew his energy and interest were limited.

"Am I disturbing you?" I asked lamely, after playing him the briefest bit.

"You're disturbing me just perfectly."

It was hot for October. I walked down the Avenue in the stultifying heat. On the Avenue are many remnants of its grandeur. And everywhere remnants of your life. That was where my mother took her dry cleaning. This was where my mother took me to Dr. Zurich for his bizarre sinus treatments. Bunny Claverie, strangely intimidated by her older sister, Blondie Claverie, lived together lifelong in that duplex on the corner. This was where I'd get my coffee after visiting my father in the hospital and then walk up to the parade when it was Mardi Gras time.

The chimes of cathedrals and convents rang through the waning afternoon, as I walked through the park. Swans, ducks. Later full moon.

I went to visit my friend Walter who claims to remember everything he's ever seen or been told—the history of every house in New Orleans, who lived in it, who lived in it before that, what dramas and scandals and tragedies happened there, etc.

His father was the source of these revelations. "The D. H. Holmes building on Canal Street—that's where I sold Huey Long his green silk pajamas," his father would say. "You see that building? Dorothy Lamour taught tap-dancing there."

"Dorothy Lamour used to live there." His father would point to a window.

I asked how his father knew all this. Did he know Dorothy Lamour? Did he just make this stuff up? No, he dated her, said Walter, who is pursued by these memories. He took her to the Blue Room at the Roosevelt Hotel. Tears come to his eyes when he thinks of it, he said.

Tears of joy? I asked. No. Because he says his whole life is about regret.

"Don't look back, Del," he said. "That's all you'll ever do."

But that's what he does. His wife Julia, being a historic preservationist, does it too. But she was less virulent about it.

They kept getting in towering arguments over things like whether someone's garden was too overgrown, or whether Julia had taken a wrong turn in the road, or whether Dresden was bombed to the ground in the war.

"It's like being chained together like two mad dogs," said Walter.

That's something you don't hear every day. As a description of marriage.

You'd pretty much have to be saintly to be married to Walter.

I was telling Amelia about them later. "The thing about it is, Julia doesn't have to try to be saintly," I said. "She just is."

"It's a talent," said Amelia.

"No, it's innate. She was born that way. The goodness. She'd never have to try."

Wouldn't it be obnoxious if she were always trying?

Oh jeez, that's what I'm like. Moralizing for hundreds of pages, bestowing my wisdom.

But I just keep doing it anyway.

In point of fact, as I watch everyone here decay and/or take care of their decaying loved one, I can understand a flawed person like Walter way more than a saintly one.

Awe at Amelia's fierce devotion. Her fierce command. Talk about a general leading the troops. I would never have undertaken such an operation. How different we are.

OK, so why do we have to be the same person?

Use your brain. You have one, right?

Harry Barrow was in town and came to visit my father at the hospital. He was a man distinguished at a young age by a spectacular tragedy. His wife was killed in a car accident when she was nine months pregnant with their first child. The person who has to endure that, if he is not broken by it, is driven to overcome it in some spectacular way, compelled to pursue a course in life with more intensity than he would have otherwise, so driven is he by despair to penetrate the tragedy and find a way forward.

It might ignite the spark of genius, as with Walker Percy. It might drive him to become the world's foremost scholar of

Dante, as with Harry Barrow. Or it might drive him to memorize the entirety of Homer in the ancient Greek, as with my father. My father was a fortunate man in all respects and I would not have characterized the heartache in his life as a spectacular tragedy. But he could not forget it.

My father took my younger daughter Grace and me to Venice when she was twelve. I had an epiphany one morning in the courtyard of an ancient music conservatory laden with the grime of centuries while someone played the "Italian Concerto" by Bach on a glorious old piano. I burst into tears, and thanked God for reminding me of who I am—a person transfixed by beauty, sobbing—and prayed to be that person again. My prayer was answered, for there in the ancient courtyard I met that same odd girl I once was and reunited with her, transported by the music of the spheres.

I come across her lately with increasing frequency. I remember her well: that dazed and heedless girl, in love with a drunk, etc. But she would be OK. The thing that she is staked on can't be gotten at or violated unless by herself.

When you're young you spend a certain amount of time finding yourself; but in the middle of this journey of our life, you tend to lose your way. Probably the same amount of time it took to find yourself when you were young, is the amount of time it takes to realize that you have lost your way again and must renew the search.

2.
In-Laws

The Garden Of Wrath

MAYBE ALL FAMILIES are alike on annual beach vacations. Tense.

We used to go on an annual vacation with the in-laws to the Southern coast in August. Our destination was an island off the coast of South Carolina. I-95 was horrendous driving down from Washington on a Friday after work, the weather sweltering, the dregs of some hurricane lashing about, whipping up the Georgia Sea Islands into a frenzy. We would be enmeshed in the usual overpowering panic-striking gridlock on Route 66 past Fairfax and Vienna and Manassas, madly clamoring past the old battlefields.

The first stop on the way down was Virginia. There is a pathological rivalry between Maryland and Virginia. People from Virginia are obsessed with it and can never get over it. Maryland is almost bland compared to Virginia and its hysterical adherents.

"What did you learn in school today?" I'd ask the kids on the endless drive. The kids were little then.

"Your skin weighs more than your brain," Adelaide answered suavely.

"Wouldn't it be weird if the ceiling was on the ground?" asked Grace.

Then they had a dramatic and simultaneous attack of nausea that caused me to veer off the highway and get all uptight at the rest stop.

Virginia did cast its spell at times. On a drive along the back roads of Virginia I had come upon certain haunted glades; and in the rustling of the leaves, the way the breeze comes through, the way the light is strange and still, you know how grave a thing went on there. Haunted by a knowledge of failure and mystery. Remorse, you might think, but that's not exactly it.

"Do you know where Grace is?" I asked at the next rest stop.

"No, where is she?"

"She's in the car having a breakdown."

"Why?"

"Because she asked me if I would take her on a Disney cruise and I said no. I said I'm not a Disney person. She said but all her friends had gone on Disney cruises. I said I don't want to be like all your friends. I just want to be like myself. And I may not perform religious observations when people expect me to, either. I don't roll over and go fetch."

"So now you're really the one having the breakdown, Mom," said Adelaide astutely.

*

A storm was gaining force. But you couldn't take it seriously because it didn't have a good name. A hurricane should be named for a voluptuous formidable black woman with a don't-mess-with-me manner or a Southern matriarch who doesn't take any of your guff. Then you could take it seriously.

"The polar bears are drowning. They're drowning in the melted Arctic ice sheets," lamented Adelaide.

"I know, I know, but what do you want me to do about it? Do you want me to go up there and give them artificial respiration or perform CPR on them or something?"

"The world is coming to an end in *my* lifetime," Adelaide went on, "but not yours, so you and Dad are just basically living it up and drinking martinis in the Jacuzzi."

Here's something no one ever talks about. We didn't know about climate change until our little kids taught us. No one told us about it before then. So it's not only that we were idiots. We didn't know we were idiots.

At five thirty sharp a cacophony of crickets came on that sounded like some sort of digital alarm clock gone awry. The highway turned into a country road alongside green fields veering off into dark roads lined by palmettos until our destination was achieved, a condo in a high-rise on the beach.

The in-laws came with the trunks of their cars laden with food and meals that had been cooked in advance, as if embarking to a land in which starvation would otherwise be probable. The group consisted of two matriarchs—my mother-in-law and her sister, Aunt Beatrice—and their husbands and sons and daughters-in-law and grandchildren.

My mother-in-law was the older sister and she called the shots. I would describe Aunt Beatrice as a more normal version of my mother-in-law. My mother-in-law was sort of inscrutable. Which may have been enhanced by her film noir sensibility. She was somewhat dark and brooding. Aunt Beatrice was more mellow.

We went inside. Stan was sitting in an armchair reading the newspaper. This was Aunt Beatrice's first husband. Although divorced from Aunt Beatrice twenty years earlier, Stan was still always hanging around in this happy-go-lucky way where no one had the heart to tell him it was causing tension. Adding to the tension was the fact that Aunt Beatrice had had a new husband for decades—the irascible Henry. Henry was considered to be surly. But you might be surly too if you were constantly confronted with your wife's ubiquitous ex-husband.

When we moved to Washington I would come home and Stan would just be sitting there like part of the furniture watching a ball game or reading the newspaper.

"Think of me as a resource," he would say.

So sometimes I did—and asked him questions about Washington.

"I'll take care of it," he'd say with his eyes closed, sweating.

"Stan, are you all right?"

"I'm just taking a break."

He was a sweet-natured guy so it didn't bother me too much. If he really had to be there for some extremely odd reason, he was welcome to just read quietly while I pursued my agenda. But if you're supposed to chat all day, then it's a problem.

The annual beach trip was claustrophobic. So I must seek respite. But if you went off alone it was treason. That was the family code. If I followed my own code it was curtains. If I went off by myself on a walk it was interpreted as an insult aimed directly at my in-laws with the ruthless exactitude of a professional assassin.

"Tell me when it's a good time for me to go on a walk," I kept saying while helping my mother-in-law with dinner. Apparently there never was a good time, so eventually I went off on a short walk.

A smoldering silence reigned in the kitchen when I returned. It took decades for the chill to thaw. It was as if my inadvertent and unwitting message to the Segals was: The party's over. Like when the teacher tells everyone to stop throwing the erasers. I didn't do it on purpose. It was simply the effect of my diluting their tribe. Or maybe it was my fun-buster persona.

A conflict arose about the convection oven. A conflict arose about the air-conditioning. The frequent skirmishes embodied deeper struggles masquerading as trivial minutiae. I tried to mediate and gloss things over. "Air-conditioning is always a sensitive issue," I said supportively.

I shopped for organic vegetables. I cooked, I cleaned.

My efforts were in vain. I tried to help but was unsung. You can't win in that situation: daughter-in-law of a Jewish mother. Built-in failure must be expected.

It may be that an innate suspicion is possessed by your mother-in-law that you are the enemy, kind of. Or that you will not conform to all the requirements. Which in fact you won't. Because you're a grown woman, fully formed, not a lump of clay waiting to be molded. I do think my mother-in-law came to accept that. Pure circumstance dictated this difference between us: she was eighteen when she got married; I was thirty-five. You can mold an eighteen-year-old woman in the 1950s. Even my fierce mother and her Ivy League degrees could be molded into having an unnatural amount of dinner parties according to elaborate Southern standards in the 1950s.

My mother-in-law was a titan of duty. Just as my own mother was. They were paragons of courtesy and decorum. Whereas for some reason I'm always brooding Byronically in a corner.

What kind of person can't conform to their in-laws' code for six days? I ask myself now. Someone incapable of a minor act of courtesy. Or a strenuous act of courtesy.

The spiritual exercises of Saint Ignatius would decree that I examine my behavior to see if it is deficient. Remorse-worthy.

You list your sins—Ignatius calls them sins. Maybe more like scrupulosity in my case—haunted by small sins, too small for God to care about, but that still disturb the soul.

Jack was from the South but a different South than mine. His was less magnolia-laden and more rugged—North Carolina.

My father-in-law was irrepressible. He kept bursting into song. Usually it was a Nat King Cole song. He taught the children how to play poker. In the afternoon if there were no televised sporting events on, he played solitaire. He had a compendium of Shakespeare quotes he'd supply at apt intervals. His favorite was Lead on, Macduff—usually further adapted to Press on, Macduff—applied when perseverance was necessary, delivered in his heavy Carolina drawl.

Basically he was a nut, so all bets were off. It's much easier to deal with a nut. His droll character had always touched my heart.

He didn't emanate the waves of togetherness. He wasn't going to make those kinds of demands. Not because he sensed my awkward state. Maybe just because he was a man, assumed to have another agenda than the constant togetherness. Or maybe just because he was a nut.

The women searched for something deeper; but somehow I was scared to get trapped in its endless depths. A depth of suffering could be sensed in Jack's mother and his sister, Stella, tortured souls who seemed to absorb all the nameless lurking sorrows that the men in the family were basically too cheerful to conceive of.

At dusk I took a solitary walk amid the deafening roar of insects. The boulevard at night was luxuriant and green, amid a glamorous enclave of oaks and palms.

Stan was inadvertently driving his archrival Henry crazy, mainly by being oblivious and unnaturally cheerful. Henry retaliated by bringing a transistor radio to the porch and listening to loud hectoring business gurus during dinner. Their mutual object of contention, Aunt Beatrice, reprimanded him from time to time for being rude.

Obviously Henry wasn't exactly the most popular person in the family. Aside from being pathologically rude, it had to do with his annoying hobbies. One year it was the clarinet. He couldn't attend family events because he had to obsessively study the clarinet. Another year it was Cajun dancing. Aunt Beatrice had to go out Cajun dancing with him three nights a week. It was spiraling out of control.

Also, he was an atheist. "I cringe whenever I hear the word God," he said—which did not make him popular with the in-laws.

Everyone seemed to find him inordinately annoying. But I found him inordinately interesting.

Later my father-in-law and I discussed the Henry/Stan conflict in all its variegated dimensions. After analyzing it from all the angles, my father-in-law concluded that Henry should treat Stan and his perpetual presence with the utmost deference and consideration. I thought that was asking a lot. But I couldn't really express my views about anything to my in-laws because my views would be too foreign. Mainly my views about the practice of religion.

We were divided by a common religion.

Aunt Beatrice's sons had married Catholic girls, who innocently attempted to celebrate their Christian rituals from time to time, causing numerous tense outbursts—mild expressions of disapproval escalating into dramatic exits, slamming doors, etc.

"How was your Christmas?" people would ask, and then I'd break into a sweat and loosen my collar. "It's a long story..."

One of the Catholic girls had tried to talk to the matriarchs about doing Passover in a different way.

"What are you talking about?" said my mother-in-law darkly.

The culprit made a few suggestions relative to a less formal and less labor-intensive format, suggestions that were greeted with stark disgust.

For me these scenes were bemusing, as I had been down that street before but had come through the fire and was on the other side. I'd say it took a good fifteen years before I learned how to handle things—or how to handle my mother-in-law—the way to do things.

Her way. You do them her way.

The Catholic sister-in-law had a breakdown. Her husband tried to mediate.

"What would you like to have happen right now?" he asked, adopting a therapeutic tone.

She said she would like to get eggs to dye for Easter.

Pretty soon everyone was snapping again.

My mother-in-law's pride in who she was impressed me. But it didn't mean I was going to roll over and go fetch.

Except it did. The first time it was my turn to put on the seder, I studiously followed all the traditions of my mother-in-law. I did try to put my individual stamp on it in however infinitesimal a way. I might delete one of the eight courses possibly, I mentioned.

The response to this suggestion was that basically there was a knife vibrating in the wall next to my head.

My mother-in-law assumed that I naturally possessed her ways and influences, or would automatically adopt them. There was some kind of inability to differentiate boundaries.

There was also a clash of cultures. Louisiana, colonized by the French, eventually sold for a song by Napoleon. Napoleon was a madman, but a doomed glamour would always attach to him in Louisiana. The land was divided into parishes that all had names like Assumption and Ascension and the streets of town were named for Catholic saints. The Code Noir had originally decreed that Catholicism was the only religion.

In New Orleans the population was still overwhelmingly

French Catholic. It was to them I looked to broaden my horizons. You want to see what's out there. Like traveling to a foreign country and observing its customs, rather than imposing your perspective and biases on them.

The Catholic girls tended to be wild. Their fathers were alcoholics whose countless children (these were old-style Catholics) littered the lawn and gardens of their houses immersed in various dramas and mishaps.

I had no Jewish culture but that which is innate. If there is such a thing as Jewish culture which is innate. It did not involve actual knowledge. Complete ignorance characterized my knowledge of Judaism. I only had the spark of the outsider, something that keeps you apart from the general crowd and gives you a harder road to travel. Is that the spark of Judaism? It could be the spark of individuality or nonconformity, etc. What I'm saying is that in New Orleans my Jewish character could be discerned in contrast to the Catholics. Such traits as being sort of intellectual, bookish, studious, and basically not being drunk.

The Jews would not think to express everything by giving a party. Then too the Jews would not ordinarily be invited to the party.

From New Orleans in the spring I used to go to Grand Hotel on the Alabama coast. The hotel had been blown away by hurricanes more than once but always was rebuilt. The women had blond hair, the little girls had huge bows and smocking on elaborate dresses. Everyone had deep Southern accents, and moved at a sometimes maddeningly slower pace. They used the word *precious* a lot. "She's just precious." Their children would be well-behaved, better behaved than mine, likely. If they had a flaw, it would be that they were *too* well-behaved, conservative, sometimes lacking a spark of divine fire that had been suppressed in favor of fitting the mold.

These were the people I had grown up around, and I felt I knew who they were, which was comforting.

A giant Easter event was going on when I went there years later with my husband. A huge and elaborate buffet, bunnies sculpted in ice. I had many curious sensations about it.

I asked my husband, "What do Christians actually *feel* about Easter?"

"Maybe something similar to what the Jews feel at Passover."

"Oh, I get it. Like it's annoying."

Which was an annoying thing to say to him, because he is very devout. And I have had reason to repent of my arrogance.

Whereas the Easter thing did not annoy me because I did not really have to participate or celebrate it or get excited about bunnies sculpted in ice. It was the same attitude I had toward the people I had grown up around in general: bemused fondness, rueful winsome interest. That's the beauty of being an outsider—things don't have to annoy you as much. You don't have to be filled with the same vast annoyance for them. Because you are not a part of them. You only observe them with bemused fondness and winsome interest.

Which is exactly the attitude I should have adopted towards my in-laws.

Instead the internal argument continued. There's a fine line between courtesy and hypocrisy. Why do I have to practice our religion *your* way, why can't I practice it my way. Because my way is incredibly lame to them. They think I'm just wandering around creating my own religion. I came to know my duty and was prepared to do it, but you can't dictate how someone *feels* about a religious observance.

I consulted a Jesuit priest at Georgetown about Catholic mysteries, what are they, are there Jewish mysteries? He said if you're sick it's a mystery what ails you until you go to the doctor and get a diagnosis. But the mysteries of religion—you can't solve them. I asked him his conception of the afterlife. He said he could not believe a love so great could end. It's hard to know what that meant. And it sounded pretty sappy. Maybe it meant: If this life on earth is all there is, that renders it absurd. Or the Lord loved them so much that he gave them this life; he must love them enough to give them an afterlife too. Which sounds kind of demanding.

I don't like being fenced in, I explained to the Jesuit priest, what about my individuality. He said I should pursue why Judaism threatens me.

The wisdom of age suggests that my in-laws' observance was intended to uphold their dedication to Judaism, rather than anything else—such as an attempt to squelch my individuality.

Still the ultimate impact is how powerful Judaism was in my in-laws' family. And how it must kind of trample everything in its path and how eventually you came to realize that you must succumb to it. At least on the outside.

On the inside I could observe in my own way, and seek "the gift of faith."

One type of person makes the effort to duty and sacrifice but the cost festers within. Like me with my in-laws. Another doesn't notice the effort to duty and sacrifice because it is second nature to him, ingrained; such acts comprise his personality or nature. A dazzling consideration for others blazes through his being.

That was how I'd always thought of Jack. The ordinary things he left in his wake, like his allergy-ridden Kleenex strewn among the bedsheets, had emanated that strange radiance to me, as if they were the relics of saints.

Groves of leaning palms against the stormy Southern sea. The men discussed baseball and stock reports. The women were plagued by nerves and insomnia. Stella simmered with barely suppressed rage for complex reasons of her own.

My father in-law screamed for the waitress: "*Sweetheart!*"

Another storm was idling in the tropics heading for the Carolinas and aiming up the coast. No one knew if it would remain a tropical depression or grow in fury but it had been named just in case.

We drove home in its midst. It was darting up and down the coast like a disturbed personality or a compulsive flirt trying to decide where to inflict the worst damage.

"Mom, nine out of ten Americans aren't getting enough whole grain," Adelaide complained on the long drive home.

I was haunted by a nameless dread. And it wasn't because nine out of ten Americans weren't eating enough whole grain. It was because the future was brewing and the dread would be nameless until some years later.

2.

No one could comprehend why or how there could be a hurricane heading for Washington, as the weather was exquisitely gorgeous. One of the effusive neighbors was having a dinner party at the exact moment when the hurricane was slated to arrive—as if it were one of the guests.

The neighbors were very effusive. Purportedly many of the neighbors were spies. They were very effusive, for spies. We were invited across the street for drinks. We were invited next door. When I got home one evening and emerged from my car, the man next door simply took me in his arms and kissed me. The hugger, we called him, because he kept hugging everyone.

So it was very surprising to later learn that he was the chief of staff at the Pentagon.

There's a thing with seats of empire where people are always having parties on the eve of war, like in a Tolstoy novel.

The first thing that happens when you move to Washington is that an FBI man comes to interview you for someone's security clearance. The interview is heavily slanted toward questions about social interaction.

"How often do you entertain socially?"

"Does X seem interested in social life?"

It's funny that he kept asking about parties because I did have to go to a lot of them.

After six years in California you get used to solitude being the key to your happiness—every man for himself, alone in a wilderness, etc. No one knows you and no one cares what you do, which is strangely exhilarating. When you come back to civilization you're traumatized by normal things like going to parties or seeing rain.

I had to get security clearance to go to a party once. It was at Blair House in honor of its recent restoration by historic preservationists. A tour was led by the chief of protocol, a fragile Southerner obsessed with discretion who kept vowing never to write a book about the scandals he had seen, which he kept referring to in a veiled way. The history of the house was poignant. There was the room where Robert E. Lee was offered by Lincoln the command of the Union Army, and where he refused it. There was the room where the chandelier almost fell on the King of Morocco right after he got out of bed.

The striking thing about these places is how unprepossessing they are. The White House looks like an old hotel that needs to be refurbished, with the King of Morocco sitting in it. The decor is pretty much that of a genteel old country club that has seen better days.

At the children's school the other mothers were going off to negotiate foreign trade agreements in El Salvador or enact international treaties in Geneva. Most people in Washington were out saving the world—which made me realize I was not as altruistic. My own daughter Adelaide at age eight was out protesting for Darfur every chance she got. When not making sarcastic comments.

It was easy to get lost in Washington. That was another thing about the District. One false move and you were in Virginia. You practically had to have ESP to find your way around the traffic circles amid the statues of generals on horseback facing certain ways to express defeat or victory.

But there is a reason why everyone keeps getting lost in Washington. It was designed to confuse the enemy.

"I'm doing a background check on your husband," said the FBI agent who interviewed me. He had a calm demeanor, almost too calm. Some of his questions seemed irrelevant. What social class did I come from, what parts of town did I frequent, did my husband like his work, what was the pay, how was the morale, and strictly personal questions like how was our love life and had he ever been unfaithful.

Was all this really necessary?

Actually, it was boilerplate. Could he be blackmailed, was he a nut.

It made you paranoid. *Was* he a nut? Washington had made him power-mad. He was always doing things like having lunch with the foreign minister of Egypt. He went to the Homeland Security Christmas party. He went to the Department of the Interior Christmas party.

He said he was going to take prednisone for his weird autoimmune complaint. The side effects were energy and volatility, he said.

"If you get any more energized and volatile we're pretty much talking Napoleon."

It was the night before the dinner party in the hurricane. My daughters and I slept in the basement to avoid the towering trees and swaying power lines. Jack was out of town on business. In the morning the neighborhood children ran around the street and a few brave souls protested against poverty in Paraguay. Some of the children attempted to organize a formal protest march but as the wind began to whip up and the towering trees swayed perilously low to the ground they contented themselves with collecting supplies for the impoverished people of Paraguay from the immediate neighbors.

"Mom, the people of Paraguay are starving and all I do is go to parties," said Adelaide.

"Well if it bothers you then stop going to parties and start helping the impoverished people of Paraguay."

"But we've just done that!" said the child, choking with remorse. "We can only do so much!"

"Exactly."

The street was carpeted with fallen leaves and branches, the neighbors milled about, with that salutary air of gaiety that sometimes precedes a storm.

I had not seen many hurricanes since leaving my hometown so long since. In my decadent youth I thought they were very exciting—have a drink, watch the sky turn an odd shade of green, while the golf course looked like a ballroom and the leaves blew around like mad, revel in the electricity going out, have another drink. But the atmosphere was always apocalyptic and everything stopped. You did not pursue your normal activities like go to school, go to work, or go to dinner parties. Hurricanes would keep you from getting to college on time or cause you to wander about the golf course in a dream since it looked like a ballroom—but you knew there would be no ball.

3.

When a man loses his mother it is sometimes said that he can lose his way. Once years later Jack and I went to the Chabad. My father asked me what exactly is a Chabad. I said we'd have to ask the authorities but I had the impression it was somewhat more mysterious or mystical than a regular synagogue. Or I liked to think so. Apparently it is a Hassidic sect. Jack says they proselytize, but for me it was more like they gave helpful explanations instead of just automatically assuming you know everything.

The rabbi had a dramatic delivery, proclaiming from a high step. He had an ancient foreign accent. His stories were somewhat disjointed. He kept saying God wants an individual relationship with you. I thought: Great! I'd much rather do one-on-one.

I asked forgiveness for my apathy, lack of discipline, and lack of executive function. (Are those sins, though?) I prayed to have more thoughts—because lately I noticed I didn't have thoughts. One minute later God gave me a thought. The thought was compassion for my husband. Who might have been comforted by a wife who embraced and shared in his religious observances.

To move among families is not an easy thing. Your own family, your in-laws, etc. One day in the far future, it will all be over, and you will shake your head and—not exactly wish to be back in it, but something more insoluble. For annoyance turns to poignance in the end, and wrath to remorse, if not from the actual acquirement of empathy and insight, then from the ultimate conclusion of the play—which I of course in my callow stupidity did not foresee.

The cemetery was most unprepossessing and the temperature was ninety-two degrees, yet once you were within the gates, it was a place of great beauty and cool repose. A mighty wind kept blowing through during the ceremony. It was obviously her presence. The rabbi actually said many things providing consolation and poetic wisdom. Your presence is more real to me than your absence.

At the grave my father-in-law pointed out where his own would be, also mentioning that he had secured a third—for his daughter, Stella, in case nothing else turned up. She seemed fairly cheerful about it. She said he had already told her about it, when they went to select the coffin. Then he wrote his wife's obituary and said, "Why don't I just go ahead and write mine too while I'm at it. Would you like me to write yours?"

Maybe not.

After dinner he went over his will with my husband. That's their favorite subject, their wills. They're constantly going over their wills. In my father-in-law's case it was at least a bit more understandable, due to his age. Never has one man been so happy to plan for his own demise and remains. I guess he does not fear death. His reaction to death is to plan for it. It seemed so gallant of him.

I woke up worrying about him, though—that he would get all scuzzy being on his own—and for the intensity of his bereavement; then remembered his massive practicality, then marveled at the grace with which my mother-in-law met her end; it was as if she was born for that: dying was a thing she knew how to do above all gracefully. Which may have been enhanced by her noir sensibility, being somewhat dark and brooding. Her husband's effusive love against this setting was yet more poignant.

There are two types of men: the kind who feels that taxes, insurance, motor-vehicle registration, and other law-abiding realms of administration are his natural ken; and the kind who does not. My father-in-law was definitely the first kind. His massive practicality was legendary. For Mother's Day he gave me a fifty-ton roll of Saran wrap from Costco—a gift that would literally last a lifetime. A gift that wrung my heart.

His motives were simple: to provide for his family financially and with consideration for their frailties. What were his own needs? To see them happy, to watch televised sports, to avoid waste and excess.

Long periods of chatting with him could be trying, as his conversation was often confined to the agreement he had arrived at with his wireless provider, the terms he had negotiated with his cable company, the miracles he had worked on his problematic mattress pad, mortgage rates, insurance premiums, cars, the hardware store (his favorite place on earth) and an encyclopedic knowledge of Costco.

He kept grousing about the lost art of conversation. Which was ironic considering that he was the world's worst conversationalist. Despite his many endearing qualities.

One of which was his comportment after he lost his wife: valiant.

They had been married for over fifty years and he was gaga about her all the way. From his description of her you'd think she was a cross between Marilyn Monroe and Mother Theresa, with Albert Einstein's brain.

Six months after she died we were meant to attend a wedding in Atlanta with the grieving widower. At the last minute his own children bailed out of the trip, leaving me to come forward and accompany him still. It would have been quite understandable had I too bailed. But I did not want to leave him in the lurch. At a social setting in this passage through his grief, my assistance might be valuable.

Continued saintliness marked my character throughout the weekend.

"Pointing out your own saintliness is not that saintly, Mom," said Adelaide.

I also offered my assistance to my tortured sister-in-law, Stella, whose statuesque and flamboyant, somewhat brazen demeanor was belied by her tortured inner soul. I promised her mother at the end that I would look out for her and to this I was faithful, and Stella was grateful, though mystified, as we didn't really get along, and I did not enlighten her as to the reason for my saintly deeds. It would be too sappy to explain it. I'm still crusty, if now saintly.

Stella would ask what are my supposedly saintly deeds. OK: I don't make waves. I make no demands. The less you say, the smoother it goes. As I have learned with Stella. You keep your distance—having learned it is a kindness—because she finds me annoying.

It's boring to be a saint. Goodness is dazzling when you come across it in others. But not in yourself, since virtue is its own reward, so it's boring.

But you do have to ask yourself: Why did I wage a war against the views and practices of my in-laws, their ways and mores—as if to differentiate myself from them? It doesn't matter that the war was waged within. The result is still the same. I should not have fought that battle. Though it only raged within. That only made it worse.

The garden of wrath. It needs to be mowed.

Life used to be like an endless newsreel that kept starting over. The reel was finally about to change. The nameless dread would have a name.

The Oyster Diaries

I KNOW a certain amount about sports, mainly baseball. Last night the Rangers won the pennant, for example, and I know what the pennant is. The thing my husband finds truly poetic is sports. He's always trying to talk to me about it and explain. "Watch this play," he keeps saying, and then explaining it. Without his explanations I don't think I would appreciate the poetry in sports, though the concept is simple: it's an arena for heroes and heroics.

It's also an arena for people who are grown men, and sometimes quite old men (e.g., the coach), who take a child's game dead seriously, treat it with extreme professionalism, pay it a zillion dollars, and take it so seriously it's as if they're soldiers in a war bound for battle zones to fight for our ideals—not playing a game with a stick and a ball.

My husband approaches sports with a level of dedication normally reserved for the enactment of international peace agreements. A lot of men are like this. They experience weird levels of well-being at victory and existential despair at defeat. Maybe sports provide for them an alternate route to emotion without actual interaction, a route to the realm of poetics and sensibility without having to read a poem or have a sensibility.

Or to put it more succinctly: "Why can't he talk about his feelings?" I asked Amelia once.

"Because he's a guy."

The other night he made me watch a two-and-a-half-hour documentary about the rivalry between the Celtics and the Lakers. I had one single reaction throughout: You call this a rivalry? This is just a pale pathetic excuse for a rivalry. Because I can't process another sports rivalry.

Jack is a conundrum. I am the perfect wife for him since I have no needs and am easily suffocated and am not suffocating. Maybe I'm not needy enough. Men like needy women. Damsels in distress.

The worst things that happen, you don't see them coming. That's what makes them the worst. One of the vagaries of age is a loss of the ability to see or detect things that are right in front of you. Usually it's when you're cooking and you can't find the oregano. But it is a metaphor with a bigger meaning—like when you don't notice that your husband has turned into a Hieronymus Bosch painting.

At least you're in the real world after that, jolted out of your pathetic stupor. Like Dante, lost in a dark wood in the middle of the journey of our life, you weren't paying attention. You were so inattentive that you didn't notice your husband had turned into a Hieronymus Bosch painting. (Just take a close look at a Hieronymus Bosch painting if you're wondering what I mean.) But my desolation does begin to make a better life. It recalibrated my soul. Like: welcome to the world, the normal world of disillusionment. The loss of my ideal of him seems almost paltry in comparison.

"There is something worse than knowing the worst. It is not knowing," wrote Walker Percy. Yes, it is unsettling to discover that the man you love—or idealize—is not the one you thought he was—or the one he never was, but you embroidered him into a vast ideal, and you can't change your entire personality in one instant and stop embroidering people into vast ideals. On a field of heroes and heroics.

When I learned of his transgression I threw myself into Dante and Shakespeare, seeking to understand the world that I had failed to see. I couldn't decipher it without a guide so I took classes. The classes were at Georgetown. I tried not to talk in class because my contributions were inappropriate but the other oldsters (auditors) talked so then I did too. The kids stuck purely to the text and the question at hand, as did the oldsters. Whereas when I talk it's all about My Personality not just Shakespeare. P.S. The other oldsters totally ignore me.

The thing that always upset me about Shakespeare was the villains. Often the villain comes out on the stage first off and confides his evil plan. (Iago, Richard III.) This only makes it more excruciating when the villain carries out his evil plan and innocent people are destroyed. What emotion are we supposed to experience in that sequence other than teeth-gnashing hatred of the villain, inwardly screaming at the victims, Don't be such a moron, don't you see what's going on, etc.? I couldn't bear it, I had no patience for it. My vision was much more insipid.

Or wait a minute—maybe it's their innocence that is the agent of their destruction. Their innocence in trusting Iago. Their inability to read his heart, see him for who he is.

I for example conveniently overlooked the fact that I was an ass or that Jack was not a god or that she who I held dear was capable of stark betrayal.

How do you deal with your despair at Iago's perfidy? I asked in class. It's so depressing.

Answer: Blank silent stares (from fellow students).

Everyone looks upon him as "honest Iago," just some great guy—why are they such idiots and morons? But oh yeah, I was exactly the same way. I did not recognize the villain in my midst. Who saw that I could be exploited. In the exact same way. I had never met a Shakespearean villain before personally. The fault of my inviolable innocence, my insipid vision—the crack she got in through.

"Are there really such women?" Desdemona asks.

How oddly innocent she is, says the professor.

That was me exactly.

One day I volunteered inanely, "I am exactly like Desdemona and Othello wrapped up into one, so Shakespeare is teaching me to change and be less stupid." In Shakespeare class

I continued to broadcast my tortured public proclamations. My flaws. My woes. My uncanny resemblance to Don Quixote (embroidering everything into vast ideals). What one man sees as a crushed and tarnished pan in the road, Don Quixote sees as the Helmet of Mambrino, a noble emblem, incomparably precious.

The kids in the class were adorable. If you idealize someone, said one kid, you'll never do anything for them because they're like a fake statue. If you idealize someone they can never be who you think they are.

I did learn that, at least. At least then I could study to look at Jack without embroidering him into a vast ideal and actually just find out who he is. And on the rare occasions when I could do that I saw this: He needs to be nurtured. Hideously, someone else had to do it when I didn't.

Other than that, the new reality was that I did not know who he is. Who is he? I didn't know. It would take more than baseball metaphors to see into his soul.

I noticed he did things that Tony Soprano did. Tony wanted to buy a house on the shore, as he plainly told Carmela, "to keep the family together." It would be a draw for the kids and their friends. Which is what Jack said when he bought the beach house. So is that who Jack is? Tony Soprano?

You think it's all about ethics at first. You're the guy in the shroud with the long white beard carrying the sign that says REPENT. You're a Florentine fanatic in the fifteenth century about to immolate herself in flames for her obsessive opposition to sin. Or maybe it's the pope who decides she should be immolated in flames. I'm not sure.

There is one key bit in the Day of Atonement service alien to my ideals (and eminently dear to Jack): they want you to atone for your sins, presuming indubitably that you would sin. The weakness was expected. The evil was presumed. That's weird. You're not just some uncontrolled amoeba swimming around the universe. Are you?

In God's eyes all men are sinners. It sounds like a Hank Williams song. This is humanity. These are the sinners. God loves them too. In fact God loves them more. But the straight shooters have to be stronger.

There is a deeper truth, but this is just the first stage.

At first you think you must fight back somehow. Draw your sword. Prepare for battle. But what will you fight? You should surrender your innocence, not fight for it. Yet at first my innocence kept unintelligently advancing like the soldiers at Gallipoli, as if directed by remote uncourageous generals.

Then there was Dante. The Dante professor was different. Although Dante seems like a moralist, our professor thinks the *Inferno* is more about tragedy than evil, the psychology of sin more than the nature of evil. There is also the psychology of the blessed, not only of the damned. Dante is looking for redemption. Thus after traversing the depths he reaches the heights:

And then we came forth again to see the stars.

Not as ecstatic as Paradise. But you came to the other side.

The old idolatry, or is it gratitude, or merely the ability to love... I still feel it, thank God, despite the disillusionments—the disillusionments were so ordinary and ineluctable, I was glad I learned them, the veil was not rent from the temple without them, I was deficient without them, something was missing without them. So I was ultimately grateful, that this basic knowledge lifted the veil from the truth and recalibrated my soul with insight.

Dante has compassion for the sinners. In the end you come to that, or else it's curtains. You have to look at what it must be like to be married to you. It must be annoying. You look at all the angles. It must be that he had never loved me quite as I loved him. In some respects that is the difference in our natures. It takes a lot to disillusion an idealist. That would be another angle, an explanation of his behavior, or a bleak truth to face. You're trying to face the worst. And/or that I was an unsatisfying spouse. Self-loathing is bad, but there is a fine line between self-loathing and self-awareness.

It may sound like a dispiriting message. But it's not just can you be gallant enough to forgive—it's more like: although I possess this stark morality, deemed by the world to be boring, I will try to understand.

*

That winter the Potomac was laden with ice. At some places downtown there were soldiers wearing fatigues. Some said they couldn't discuss their mission. Others said they would go to Korea if there was a war. I drove past the embassy of the Côte d'Ivoire, a fascinating crumbling palazzo. Mysterious caravans often drove past, creating paranoid Washington moments, with black SUVs and studiously nondescript square-jawed men talking tensely into their secret earphones.

The pope was in town, causing huge traffic jams. The pope seemed to follow me wherever I went. Maybe because of the shroud.

Adelaide came home from college for Thanksgiving. "I feel so sorry for the turkeys," she said. "Just let the turkeys live."

"Your compassion for the turkeys is very beautiful but I'm cooking one. I have to read the directions. It takes hours." Grace cooked a pasta dish for lunch while we were waiting.

"I loved the pasta, Grace," I kept saying over and over. "Let me tell you how much I enjoyed the pasta," I continued. "This pasta you made is exquisite."

"Mom you're driving me crazy."

So the holiday was gotten through, Adelaide went back to college, and Grace navigated her last year of high school while simultaneously conducting her wastrel youth. And I looked for opportunities to discuss the crisis when I was alone with Jack, or to find out what I did not know by what I did—like the Duke of Wellington standing on the hill.

At the bus stop to New York while seeing Adelaide off, I felt a pang of psychic weakness to anticipate the melancholy of eternal partings from one's children, and then walked home along the mildly charming byways of the greensward. But it turns out the intervals between parting from one's children are not so bad. You get used to it.

After throwing myself into Dante and Shakespeare I threw myself into reading the Bible.

Then I had to do my Daily Record of Dysfunctional Thoughts. As instructed by the shrinks.

But in the end I fled to New Orleans to escape the winter and the pain and the cause of the pain: Jack. One story is of the woman who leaves and doesn't worry about whether or not he'll come after her. In a way that's what was happening then. Only when you give up hope are your hopes realized. Or to love less is to suffer less? Or as Dante would have it, through suffering your soul is made.

My father had a mental crisis in Italy in 1954, after his soul received the shock from which it never fully recovered.

"He went around like a zombie for years," said the transgressor, my mother.

There is a striking similarity about our lives in this respect—my father's and mine.

I sympathized instantly with my mother, that is not the

tragic part, but that my father took it so hard. His ability to be consoled by Latin fricatives and Greek macros (whatever that is) developed then, driven by the heartache he never got over. For me it was Dante and Shakespeare. For him it was ancient Greek and peat stacks and stuccators.

So it came to be that having fled the pain, having traversed some realms of Shakespeare and Dante to escape it, one day I was in my father's study. He was at his desk. I stood behind him while he showed me the bookplate designed for him by a New Orleans architect in 1954.

I asked him to explained its elements.

His Latin motto, which he translated as: Persevere, it suits you—was the rubric over the design. The exact translation is: Persevere, it is fitting, for a better fate awaits the afflicted. My father's translation is more suave, though the other more exact. The line is from Virgil, the *Aeneid*.

In my mother's papers I found a note he wrote on June 11, 1953: "Claire flew off today to spend six weeks in the tropics for a rest cure in Nassau." I found the adoring letters he wrote to her while she was there. The adoring letters are not dated. Which was striking since I knew him as one to insist that every article of writing be prefaced by the date. It was while he wrote these adoring letters that it happened—the cataclysm in his life by which he would thenceforward date all things.

Everything thereafter must be marked out by a date, so as

to always be alert to the passage of events, the sequence of their history.

As one must then begin, patiently and painfully, as he had learned in the army, to "appreciate the situation."

Worse that he poured forth his love and his concern for her in these adoring letters while it was happening unbeknownst to him. The similarities are so curiously exact in some respects—his trusting adoring love. How I used to idolize Jack.

Tears were streaming down my face silently as I stood behind him. He did not know my story, though I knew his. I wanted to confide in him, to teach him there are explanations and that understanding can be sought. But a man is less likely to forgive, to allow for human foible.

He never forgave her. He said he didn't. But they lived together for the next forty years until he showed her through the door to heaven.

"I don't think you could have done that if you didn't love her," I said.

"My father helped me," he said. "He knew my story. He gave me his advice."

"What did he say?"

"This is a test of *your* character."

An enigmatic comment.

Below the Latin motto on the bookplate there was a drawing of the best oyster he ever ate, on April 4, 1952.

Following that were the sugarcane fields at Bayou Lafourche, to signify where his father was born and where his family began in Louisiana.

His father, Ever Anhalt, was the last of nine children and led the family when they lost their parents. "Some boys are men before they turn twenty-one," he said to his many brothers when that time came. "And that is what we must be." He was ten years old. It was curious to have a boy of ten calling the shots, but Ever Anhalt was the family prodigy. He went to college when he was fourteen—the first in his family to go that far. He went to law school in the North three years later.

In 1907 he returned to found the law firm DeGaullier & Anhalt in New Orleans. DeGaullier had the money and social position. Anhalt had the brains. The clients were heavy hitters, including United Fruit, Coca-Cola, the Port of New Orleans, and the Louisiana Rice Milling Co. My father inherited these clients.

Usually people go out into a world that is more glamorous than the one that they have left. This wasn't really the case in my father's generation. They went off to colleges and wars and then came home to work beside their fathers and grandfathers. With my father it was the same. He went to World War II, to law school in the North, and then returned to practice law beside his father, bringing home with him a Yankee bride. He bought a bungalow in the Black Pearl, and when his father died, moved back to the house he was born in.

The Black Pearl was like all New Orleans neighborhoods—segregated but adjacent to a neighborhood of the other race. It was situated between the Avenue with its grandiose mansions and a bend of the Mississippi River uptown comprising a modest black neighborhood. Between these two the edges bled together slightly more than was usual—into the Black Pearl.

It was daring of August Anhalt to have bought a house there, perhaps influenced by the Yankee bride. I would walk to the black church on the corner with Franciola, who took care of me when my mother was away having her breakdown.

Sometimes we drove to the Gulf Coast. Franciola was not allowed to stay in the hotel on the Gulf Coast unless she was wearing her uniform. My childhood conception of Franciola was that she was an intrinsically sweet and excellent woman who would wish to serve with grace because that is the person she was, the character she possessed—despite whatever obstacles I vaguely sensed had come her way. I was a Blanche DuBois in training. The naked bulb would always be too harsh.

But a dim ray of shame developed, an innate refrain, that I was unworthy of Franciola and others in our house with whom my relationships as the years went by were not really jovial or jocular as in the conventional cliché, but instead quite awkward and embarrassed and self-conscious. There was something extremely odd about it.

That a Yankee girl with high ideals should be asked to come

into this world and administer it—the elaborate staff in my father's house and the starkly separated gradations of society in New Orleans—would seem to be asking a lot. But Claire Anhalt definitely got the idea. And not only that, but in a defining moment for the Yankee bride, Technique (the butler) informed her one afternoon, with dignity, that he was in love with her.

She coolly met his gaze and suggested that he should now be sweeping the entrance hall.

If someone was having a breakdown, sobbing in the anteroom, ordinarily you would expect the other party to say, Darling what's wrong, or take them in their arms, or step around and give them a hug, a pep talk, etc. Or if someone was pouring their heart out or declaring their love, you might expect the other person to kindly explain why they could not return your love. Maybe only a Yankee could summon such stiff-necked businesslike force, forget the layers of history and shame, and simply pursue the program with resolve—whether it was with an employee or a daughter.

Hers was a democracy of criticism, equally distributed among all; and hers was a force to be reckoned with, more than a love to be sought.

We had a lot of weird relatives. Uncle Junior, a lifelong bachelor, tormented his mother throughout her life by materializing out of a dark hall daily at the cocktail hour, his remarks soaked in sarcasm. He had a sort of fallen Barrymore matinee idol profile, if John Barrymore looked really seedy, which he actually kind of did.

Aunt Baby married a devastatingly handsome man after knowing him for two weeks. He was prone to stray. And when he strayed, he *really* strayed—to Shanghai, India, Madagascar—for months at a time. During his absences she would decamp to her mother's house. She always talked like she was about to give a party. "Are you ready for this, kiddo? It's congestive heart failure!" her jazzy way of talking investing the most tragic events with gaiety.

Their mother, Alice Anhalt, was a straight shooter, a hectoring moralist, sober and punctual and puritanical in every way, in stark contrast to her ubiquitous children.

I would observe these characters with bemusement while I was growing up. It was quite intriguing: Your children kept going mad and then had to live with their mother for the rest of their lives, like in a Tennessee Williams play.

Alice Anhalt walked down the Avenue every morning at the age of ninety-five dressed to the nines in her hat and veil and fur, leaning on her cane.

"I have decided to live in the past," she announced one day in 1960.

New Orleans decided to do pretty much the same thing. You could kind of hear things having come to a screeching halt in some previous epoch.

*

In the early 1950s my father inherited United Fruit as a client and went to the site of the operations once or twice and brought my mother, who had a fondness for the tropics. The jungle, the green, the bemusing hopelessness. Charismatic dictators. Problems. The mystery of the tropics. New Orleans had given her a perfect breeding ground for observation in psychology. The tropics gave her more.

The banana company had come to the deepest stifling hopeless place and provided thirty years of excitement and false prosperity and when it left, the place would drop back into its hopeless forgotten-ness, but somehow worse—like in a Gabriel Garcia Márquez novel. Then everything would go back to the troubled picturesque solitude as before. That's the mystery of the tropics. New Orleans was the same.

Among my father's effects is a very curious item. It's an oyster diary, where he grades the oysters at the Pearl, a restaurant downtown, across the street from his office. He had lunch there every day. It starts in January 1954, and is plainly an attempt to come to grips with what he said was the hardest year of his life. Each entry is preceded by the date, a grade, and then a terse description in a miniscule scrawl. It is the work of a madman.

Sept. 2—awful
Sept. 4—still awful
Sept. 5—terrible
Sept. 7—no good
Sept. 10—terrible
Sept. 12—wonderful
Sept. 13—miserable
Sept. 17—exceptional
Sept. 18—very poor
Sept. 19—passable
Sept. 20—fabulous
Sept. 21—utterly tasteless
Sept. 22—beautiful to look at but no salt
Sept. 28—very fine
Sept. 29—not so hot
Sept. 30—lousy
Oct. 1—unusually fine
Oct. 3—not yet
Oct. 5—not ever yet
Oct. 6—not ready yet
Oct. 7—at last!
Oct. 8—even better
Oct. 9—still magnificent
Oct. 10—superb
Oct. 11—declined slightly

Oct. 13—still flat
Oct. 14—beautiful but tasteless
Oct. 15—marvelous
Oct. 16—unbelievable
Oct. 17—warned away

It goes on that way for twenty years.

My mother used to say that he was shutting things out. "He's shutting out the mayor," she would say. (The mayor was also shutting things out, she noted, since he was in the process of being defeated by a landslide but was throwing a huge victory party.)

My father shut things out with Latin fricatives, ancient Greek, etc.

Someone (actually Jack) said that getting married is like playing musical chairs. You marry who you're sitting next to when the music stops. Not the most romantic view. But you don't want to be the last one at the dance. I was the belle of the ball at one time. And when the belle leaves the ball, what happens? The madness ceases and all is quiet. Why? Because there's no more hope for the other men at the ball.

At some point in her life every woman experiences renunciation. Many women experience it to some extent upon marriage, others long before.

Jack wasn't obligated to love me, I had realized long before. I had regarded him as a saint in many respects and would have to be on my toes to be worthy. I must renounce some things for him. His love might not answer all of my needs, but would answer the main one, and so I would renounce the others. I mean how else is it going to work?

Amelia was the first person I told after Jack disclosed to me the truth. She did not appear overtly shocked—being more worldly and possibly more acquainted with subterfuge than me—and she would rather have been submerged in a vat of boiling oil than desert her defense of Jack. She was like a nineteenth-century Frenchwoman in a Balzac novel. She provided her usual weirdly outmoded spiel from another generation—or century: "Don't show him how you really feel, don't show anger, don't drive him away, be strong, show him your strength, act totally serene."

"I'm not a professional actress."

2. Bad Oyster

You probably want some details. You want to hear the whole sordid story, maybe.

It is too sad to tell. It makes you mentally nauseous to think of it.

We were in New York when he told me. It was early June. We were at a hotel. The palaces of Manhattan were all around us. Skyscrapers instead of greenery. It gave me the creeps. He said he had done something terrible. He put his head in his hands. There were long tortured silences. Finally he came out with it.

At first the drama seemed unreal. Like when the teacher tells everyone to stop throwing the erasers and no one listens amid the uproar. And I'm usually the one who tells everyone to stop throwing the erasers. And there was no uproar. Unless it was the huge waves of my innocence crashing on the shore.

It was so outlandish that I kept thinking that he had a brain tumor causing temporary insanity.

"Does anyone else know?" I asked. Because other people close to us were involved.

"Yes. Our daughters."

Jesus Christ.

"How?"

"Grace asked to use my phone one day and discovered texts, she confronted me; she took pictures of the texts and sent them to Adelaide. Adelaide invited me to dinner in New York pretending everything was normal, acting super nice. When I walked into the restaurant the proverbial knife was vibrating in the wall next to my head."

Speechless shock.

"Are they able to forgive you?"

"Adelaide says she never wants to speak to me again unless it's about logistics. Grace is more psychologically probing about it. But she made me tell you."

A piteous collateral sorrow that a seventeen-year-old daughter on the brink of life had to make this discovery. Though if not for her psychological genius in making him tell me, my idiotic innocence would have been lifelong preserved.

The next morning I took the train back to Washington praying I would not run into Ivy when I got there. The train was standing-room only and would only go ten miles an hour. After crawling at one mile per hour to Philadelphia I gave up and got out and went across the track and found another train, also standing-room only, which was filled with an inordinate number of priests.

Why are there so many priests on this train, I wondered, and kept accidentally stepping on their cassocks.

Looking back I observed things involving Ivy that to anyone literally possessing a brain would point in one exact direction. It's not necessarily that I was incapable of putting two and two together, although there was that; it was more that I knew she was annoying, but I had always loved her, and was devoted to her.

The trouble with the weak is that you have to protect them. The strong don't need to be protected. The weak take advantage of you—not necessarily even deliberately or consciously but through lack of tact, lack of insight. And after they have taken advantage of you, then you have to protect them.

But why, Del, why? Because you're so magnanimous? Because you are strong? Or because you're a doormat.

"You don't introduce your girlfriend on a flying trapeze to a hundred of your friends and relatives for no reason," observed Aunt Beatrice when the family was summoned to London to meet Ivy.

"That's true. But most people I know don't have a girlfriend who is a flying-trapeze artist," I said. "If they did, they would probably do that."

"Maybe there will be an announcement," continued Aunt Beatrice. Regarding her son's prospects. "An engagement."

There was. The wedding of Albert and Ivy one year later took place at the northernmost tip of Scotland. I took a windswept evening walk along the bracing North Sea with Adelaide and Grace, then aged eight and twelve. I went for cocktails in the castle. You could pick out the bride's friends—fellow trapeze artists and contortionists—by their general profile and demeanor: they had names like Jezebel and wore outlandish frocks.

In the morning I was summoned by the bride to help edit her marriage vows (Sweetheart give me rewrite). By then we were fast friends.

Albert had lived in Europe for twenty years working at an international investment bank. Most of his deals were in Italy and all of his previous girlfriends were Italian. They were always yelling at him. Sometimes his family had worried about the psychological ramifications of these relationships but Jack explained, "Basically if you're Italian and you're not throwing a plate of fruit at someone's head, you should check your pulse."

And the volatility factor would now be moot, I thought, given the inane clichés of British restraint that I subscribed to.

"So they're coming in September," said Aunt Beatrice when their move to the USA was planned. "And they'll stay with you until they find a house."

"Maybe they should rent an apartment until they find a house," I said.

But that was not the family ethos.

So when I got home from teaching my class in Baltimore one day in September, my open-ended houseguests and their baby and their seven steamer trunks were littered everywhere, having made the move from London.

Sobbing was heard. Not the sobbing of an infant.

At night there was more sobbing and more tortured one-sided arguments.

Talk about someone who was traumatized. From the moment Ivy landed on our shores she fell completely apart and became hysterical. I was extremely surprised at her behavior because of my rabid Anglophilia and demented conceptions of the British character. Obviously you have sangfroid if you're going to swing from a flying trapeze suspended over a concrete floor. Obviously that takes an iron nerve. So where was the proverbial stiff upper lip?

While trying to prepare for my teaching duties every day I would attempt to pretend that Ivy was my grown daughter having a nervous breakdown so it might seem more normal to imagine her and her baby lurking just outside my office doing laundry, acting needy, and making signs of coming in to chat.

"I can't chat right now," I said gruffly when she crossed the line into my office.

"That's an interesting outfit you're wearing," said Ivy.

"I can't talk right now," I said, as I did not have time to explain my outfit.

"It was just a comment," said Ivy.

I hoped she didn't find my gruffness offensive. I need not have worried. The person Ivy found offensive was her husband Albert.

Ivy was the type of person who liked to wrangle with waiters.

"Could you bring us something other than soggy bread?"

"This is inedible."

"Could I have some non-swamp water please."

"She sounds like an ass. Why do you like her?" said Amelia.

"I love her. She's effervescent. Fizzy. Witty."

*

"Mom, how long are they staying?" said Adelaide.

"Until they find a house."

"Do they have to stay till then? She's awful."

"What? She's adorable."

Children and dogs, they have sharp instincts. The girls understood something that I never did.

Ivy's violent disaffection with her husband continued to escalate after they found a house of their own around the corner. Her aim became divorce. But Albert wouldn't let her go, and Ivy wasn't satisfied with the financial settlement he came up with from time to time in a half-hearted gesture of surrender.

That had been the situation for some time when Jack made his shocking disclosure to me.

Until that day she and I remained fast friends. This was to some extent the most shocking part, that I could be the dupe of the universe in that way. She constantly asked my advice while delivering her litany of woes. Every Monday evening we took long walks and went out to dinner.

I loved hearing her complain incessantly about "your bloody country" for two years. I loved hearing her complain incessantly about Albert. He had to brush his skin and meditate and hang upside down on a transverse lumbar contraption in the morning before he could help their daughter or talk to Ivy about her needs. Albert was limited, I told her. Most people are.

I tried to empathize; I pondered Ivy's "noble struggle" to get free.

BECAUSE I AM THE WORLD'S LITERALLY MOST STUPID PERSON.

Albert may have had to brush his skin and hang upside down to find the strength to cope, but he, like me, was an innocent. I found their situation annoying for its endless lack of resolution, but I tried to analyze it closely to determine if it really was annoying or if, like Ivan Karamazov, I was base. I could always find ignoble motives in myself. I searched in vain to find them in others.

I went on to chastise myself for ignobility. I must be magnanimous and help Ivy in her struggle.

CLUELESSNESS TRAINING AVAILABLE HERE

The moralist asks herself what the good person would do, and has to force herself, sometimes, to act in that way. But she doesn't really have to force herself. Her more immediate concern is remorse when even her feelings are ignoble, although she knows that while you can control your actions, you cannot control your feelings. And she will always search herself for blame before she blames another.

THE CREDO OF THE SAPSUCKER

*

"Shall we go look at the cherry blossoms?" said Ivy. "We can take Stella and Aunt Beatrice when they visit."

"I really don't see what the big deal is about the cherry blossoms," I commented.

Cherry blossoms and giant pandas—people were always raving about how enchanting they are. I've never seen one group of people so obsessed with giant pandas.

"Aside from your enmity to the cherry blossoms, it would be a family activity for Stella and Aunt Beatrice and the girls."

I let it drop. I would let the suggestion marinate. Maybe they would go without me.

Why were we always wrangling? I assumed it was because of Ivy's domineering personality.

In reality I guess it was me standing in her way.

It would be annoying enough, Ivy's behavior, even without the knowledge I later learned of her ungodly actions going on in secret. But in light of what she was really doing at the time—it is beyond what can be understood.

At least it was beyond what could be understood by me.

"How's Jack?" asked Ivy before we parted.

"Well, you know, when you've been married twenty-five years, it's kind of like a Walker Percy novel," I said vaguely.

"How's the tennis?" Ivy asked. It was our code word for sex.

"Right, it's been a long time, the longest it has ever been, I need to work on that..."

Thus the dupe, whose nature is so far from doing harm that she suspects none.

Ivy was ten years younger than me and people kept mistaking me for her mother at her wedding two years earlier. But my confidence in what I saw as my intrinsic glamour had always been strangely secure. Despite my librarian-like presentation. A plain Jane—Why, Miss Jones, you're beautiful!

Maybe it was another quixotic delusion. Former glamour girl and now deposed matriarch.

"How was it possible?" I inappropriately asked my seventeen-year-old daughter, doubtless already irreversibly traumatized by her discovery of the texts, but more insightful than marriage counselors or shrinks.

"He's about to lose his last child to adulthood, both daughters out of the house, he's scared or doesn't know how to proceed..."

"Have you been diagnosed as a certified genius?" I asked her.

"I watch a lot of movies."

I stopped to watch her apply makeup with the surgical precision of a highly trained bomb-defuser, and felt momentarily renewed.

*

"Why are you so calm and gracious, Del?" asked Louise Brown. "I'd go straight to her door and say 'If you come near any member of my family, I will destroy you.'"

This was bemusing advice. The bemusing part was the contrast between Louise Brown's saintly Catholic ways, her Southern butter-wouldn't-melt-in-her-mouth demeanor, and her iron wrath. It was not my way. But it was food for thought.

Before I fled to New Orleans the iron magnolias urgently advised me to make such declarations as the above in no uncertain terms. The iron magnolias were incensed with rage at the suggestion of a particle of sympathy for Ivy. I was the dupe of the entire universe. Galaxies included. But in the end I told myself that I could not control everything. I don't make blanket prohibitions to control everyone. I don't control people. I don't issue commands.

But maybe that was just another way of saying "I have had my backbone surgically removed."

"She keeps texting me," said Jack's sister, Stella, who was visiting him while I was in New Orleans. "I don't know whether to let her visit me. Here at your house."

A temporary backbone had been surgically inserted in my spine so I delivered a more unequivocal answer.

"It's not a good idea," I said on the advice of the iron magnolias. "That's all I know."

It felt forceful. The iron magnolias were incensed with a chorus of rage.

But you can't control how people feel. You can only try to work with it. What did I do, possibly, to make someone behave this way toward me; what is humanity, etc.

The temporary backbone was corroding.

Winter was coming, as they say in *Game of Thrones*. I had not yet fled to New Orleans. Winter in Washington can be towering—as in that painting of George Washington sailing across the Delaware in a massive snowstorm.

Like George Washington, I could not tell a lie. But unlike George Washington, my hair was a disaster and my soul was filled with darkness. It was January. I was conducting my twenty minutes per day of interrogation and analysis.

Sometimes I had trouble believing his words—even when the words were "I love you, I love you, I love you," as he kept saying over and over on our wedding night twenty-five years earlier. To me his words had sounded insincere. He was drunk. I have a phobia of people when they can't hold their liquor. That's why he calls me the fun-buster.

"You look like Lord Kitchener finding the First Lord of the Admiralty's report unsatisfactory," he said.

Yeah. Duh.

Or maybe it was just my vibe. My fun-buster persona.

And what about his vibe. How cruel it sounds.

He was studiously rereading one of the generic books I had lent him. This book was unintentionally hilarious while being biblically instructive. It was addressed to the betraying man who wanted to get his wife back. It was written from the perspective that your wife is an incomprehensible creature who it would be impossible to communicate with unless you learned a set of alien specifications and precise instructions regarding how to pacify her, how to answer her questions, and if this was all too difficult to grasp, scripted speeches were included at the end, with cautions not to sound as if you'd memorized them. But from this ludicrous framework came a message of resolve and exactitude. The only way forward.

"Are you ready to put this behind you and move on, Del?" asked the marriage counselor.

"No I'm not ready. Are you joking? And give up all this—the cross-examinations, the tortured speculations, the plea for repentance, the search for clues, the prosecution of the case, the—"

The in-laws would be coming to visit soon and I would be drowning in a sea of pathology. I would have to hold it together. Like a Southern matriarch with a family crisis and a party to host. But the cut is deeper. I would be like the Duke of Wellington on the battlefield watching his general lose his leg and still cheering on the troops.

Later I was driving home and there had been a storm. The atmosphere was ominous and violent. The car radio was playing a familiar and dramatic piece of classical music that was also ominous and violent. I struggled to identify it—Brahms? Mahler? Finally, on the streets of Chevy Chase in the storm-washed winter greensward, I realized it was the score from *Swan Lake.*

I had taken Ivy to that ballet while unbeknownst to me the infamy was going on. I had been so easy to deceive.

It galvanized anew in me the need to try to ascertain: Where was I? Where the hell was I?

If Jack seems missing from this story it is because I did not know who he was. I'm trying to figure it out. He keeps talking about the debt ceiling. "The stock market is an institution dedicated to truth," he says. OK, so scary tycoon stuff? "It's emotional. It gets mad. It goes down much faster than it goes up because that's when it discovers that it has been lied to. A stock can be overvalued for a while but ultimately the market will find its truth."

So it's a giant metaphor for everything. The stock market. And/or another conversation in code, like sports.

Maybe he was protecting me, with his drugstore Indian keep-mum persona. More likely he knows there's no good in this story and as if being evaluated by the all-knowing stock market, the truth had come out. The value diminished.

*

"Mom, you can't talk about this with your daughters, you have to stop, we are going out into the world, we want to do it with some shred of optimism."

Ouch.

Fair enough. I was trying to learn it but kept accidentally forgetting. I would soon learn.

"At least I'm not wearing a black lace slip and drinking vodka."

"Do you have a therapist, Mom?"

"I had one but she was illiterate and tedious and annoying so I had to get out of it."

While watching *Game of Thrones* I came across the female knight who goes around pledging herself to protect her charge—a king, a queen, or just some random person. The touching thing about it is her goodness. Her only path in the world is to conduct this stated purpose with the utmost excellence.

I'm not a fourteen-year-old boy, so why am I watching *Game of Thrones*? Is there a fourteen-year-old boy inside of me somewhere? Maybe, but I don't think that's it. I ignore the blood and gore part to focus on the steadfast goodness of certain characters and the nobility of others.

There is a difference between goodness and nobility. A good

person is always good; his goodness is neutral, for it is constant and unchanging. Whereas nobility implies an element of renunciation. The noble person made more of a sacrifice because it was not in his nature to sacrifice. He had to make more of an effort.

You're still looking back, over the big picture, from day one. When I was twenty-five I moved to New York from New Orleans. I went on dates with total strangers who were writers and journalists and humor writers. There was one who made me laugh all the time; after all, he was a humor writer. Actually they were all humor writers. Each one broke my heart, each one in a different yet hauntingly similar way. So at first I was in raptures but later in despair. They could always tell the difference. It wasn't hard. You wore your troubles on your sleeve, as plain to the observer as the color of your shoes.

We met in Times Square for a drink. There was a huge blizzard going on. I did not know whether you were still supposed to go to parties you had been invited to if there was a huge blizzard going on. I had a secret gaiety. I was riding his bike in Times Square while he walked beside me and it broke in the middle of Broadway and he then tried to fix it. I was in stitches. We had to put it in a taxi. I was laughing my brains out. He kept saying, in his wry way, just sitting there on the whole other side of the seat, "I think you ought to spend the night with me. I think you ought to let me come with you. Can I spend the night with you."

"No, no," I said, laughing my brains out, with the broken bike in the trunk. He came to my apartment and we talked, but I didn't have to talk—I just stood at the window looking out at the huge blizzard because I had never seen one before. He just sat there staring at me. He wanted to do more things, he said. Sooner or later we did the things and he was very brave to persist with me, because I was a demented cross between Scarlett O'Hara and Lord Byron. Time went on and he bravely persisted until the well of his bravery had run dry, and I was a broken, shattered person who went on more dates with New York boys who were total strangers and who were humor writers. We met at the Rialto. We met at the Odeon. I cried the whole way there on the bus. I cried the whole way home in the taxi. It kept going on like that for ten years. It was like that until I met Jack.

"You just have to find someone who will put up with you," Walker Percy used to tell me. It may not sound romantic but it had the ring of truth. This was the broken road that led to Jack.

The most able in a family helps the others. That was pretty much Jack's role in his. He was the fixer of the family. He paid their bills, if necessary, he restructured their debt, he funded accounts for their childrens' college education.

He had fixed me too. But since the exact moment of making his disclosure he had lost his personality. He acted wooden.

As a consequence of his sad tortured lost-soul demeanor I often felt compelled to minister to him—instead of the reverse. As if I had to be the strong one or was not the injured party.

I asked what was bothering him now. He claimed that what was bothering him was Adelaide wanting to quit her job in order to devote herself to fighting racism. If you're upset about her devoting her life to fighting racism then maybe it means you are a racist.

"I feel guilt and sadness at how I ruined everything," he said. He was gloomy, deadened and wooden. He seemed gripped by nostalgia. "I don't want to lose you because I love you and you are my vision of truth," he said in his tortured wooden way. "You face the truth head-on. The consequences may be awful but you would rather confront them than avoid them. I have met few who had this courage. And honesty."

"Really? Where have you been living, Alcatraz?"

"I want things to be like they were before, Del," said Jack. "I want to go back to that."

"It can never be what it was before. That's over. It has to be something different. For me it will be better. My life won't be a quixotic delusion."

I straggled into the marriage counselor's like a sad old person. I felt like a slug. I felt old. "How are you, Del?"

"I feel old."

"How about you, Jack?"

"I feel deadened."

"You're cured!" said the marriage counselor inexplicably.

She turned to me. "You've made so much progress."

"I have?"

"You've both done so much work. You're stable now."

"We are?" It was so weird. "I had a vision of corruption," I said. "Ivy probably would have expected everything to just go back to how it was before, when we were all inseparable—as if nothing. That was the vision of corruption she could have lived with. And by the way, why did she never ask for my forgiveness?"

"Because she's not sorry," said the marriage counselor.

Having your brain surgically removed meant that you would never think of that yourself. That our friendship could have meant so little to her and been so easy to sacrifice. That the stakes were higher if she won with Jack than if she lost with me. And now she's swum far off into the sea where I can never reach her, and where I now realize that I never could.

And what's the deal with the weird fake frozen smile? The one she has when she sees me. When I run into her in the neighborhood, as I pray I never will, but as I occasionally would. It makes her look like a different person from the one I knew. More cunning than any creature in the field.

"You need to get your things for college, Grace," I said.

"Mainly I have to go to Bed Bath and Beyond to get stuff for my dorm room."

"What's the *beyond* for, I wonder. Bedding, towels—and the galaxy? Do they have shower curtains in the Andromeda Strain?"

"It's for bed, bath, and kitchen."

"But instead it has to be a huge euphemism. Like you can't say *kitchen*. It's too blunt. You have to use this huge euphemism—Beyond—like beyond the galaxy."

"I think it just means a realm of mediocre knickknacks and random pots and pans," said Grace. "Calm down."

Then she went off to conduct her wastrel youth and climb the steep hill that would lead to all the years ahead, armed with the salutary loss of innocence that had escaped her loving, unusual mother.

My father had a recurring dream: He was in Italy, at a crossroads; in one direction was a village with a hill; in the other direction—nothing.

One road led to interest/aspiration and the other to nothing/nowhere. It was pretty obvious which road you would take, right? The idea, to me, was that you had this choice—

"This is a test of *your* character."

Why do I still love him? Is that the test of my character?

Love in the Ruins

The past is a foreign country; they do things differently there.

—L. P. HARTLEY

THE GOOD THING ABOUT AGE is being a straight shooter with no time for falderal, so you can impart your wisdom—not imperiously, but just more like: Someone has to say it and it's going to be me.

When can we get off this mad carousel, I sometimes wondered in my wastrel youth. There was the sensation: This is going to be a disaster but somehow I'm letting it happen. I know how it's going to end—not well—but I was like those people in the movies who are paralyzed though can still see everything that is going on. We were experts at the narrow escape.

As was New Orleans itself.

One day when I was twenty-four I was speeding down the Avenue in a wastrel trance beneath the green arcade of oaks. Another driver who appeared to be stopped at the neutral ground proceeded to cross the street and we collided. Shockingly, it was his fault—or at least so he kept wildly declaring to all the bystanders, witnesses, friends, and police. I emerged unscathed.

Claude Collier instantaneously appeared on a motorcycle in a black suit. He was the blue-eyed boy with the crooked smile. Dangerously elegant, acquainted with trouble, he threw down the motorcycle and came over to me. Storm Durant was driving down the Avenue then, so she also stopped. Gin Allstrom somehow arrived. Various bike riders from the park wandered over. Basically, people from all over town showed up. A jazz band practically played.

Gin Allstrom took me to the hospital, although I was unscathed. Claude followed on the motorcycle. At the emergency room he kept following the nurses around saying, "She's in pain. This is ridiculous." They made him leave.

A pivotal moment occurred the next day. My mother took me to lunch at the Pontchartrain Hotel. She begged me to take measures to restructure and redirect my life, which she said was sinking into a quagmire of unreality and lack of purpose. She told me I was living in a dream world.

I could tell that what my mother said was true. I could recognize or sense it very distinctly: I was living in a dream world.

My mother's face at fifty-four was lined and tired. There was a weariness in her demeanor and her gait. But at the same time it was a face with great character and still very beautiful. Her eyes—her green eyes—were clear and refreshingly green like the sea.

It was abundantly plain to her that the world and most people in it, especially her daughter, were crumbling into a state of decay and atrophy and blight.

Again she was correct. Something with this life you were leading was very wrong—except you did not know what it was. It was a nameless wrong. This nameless wrong followed you wherever you went but you could not put your finger on it.

The youth has not yet met his destiny and does not know how it will all turn out for him. And the youth is haunted by that mystery.

It hasn't panned out yet. The defining moment has not yet come.

Meanwhile there was some sort of fashion show going on and during this whole conversation models kept stopping by our table to say, "I'm wearing a sequined gown from Givenchy..." or "This is a tailored Chanel dress suit with pearl buttons."

"You've got to pull yourself together," said my mother.

"I'm wearing a sharkskin skirt and matching jacket," said the model standing at the table.

"The people you associate with are dragging you down," she said.

But it didn't do to argue.

"They're wild and they're lightweights, and Claude Collier is blazing the trail."

The battlefield awaits. I must contend with this onslaught.

"He's pathetic, Delery," said my mother.

"Not everyone can be normal. Completely normal. I mean at all times."

My mother knew the case looked difficult. The hippie girl in the odd green dress who sat across from her was plainly going another route from the one society prescribed. It was chillingly ironic that the fashion show had been going on during the conversation, because her daughter did not dress correctly, she did not wear lipstick, and her hair was not well coiffed. In short she was unkempt. That was not the only difficulty. There is a fine line between unkempt and nihilistic.

It wasn't a deliberate choice of mine to go outside the confines of decorum. That came later. At first it was a failure so intrinsic that it would not have occurred to me to conform. In fact it never would. Yet a weird despair came of not fitting in.

I imagined that my mother and her social milieu felt disgust at my failure to measure up to their standards of suavity and comportment. I had once been like them: well-dressed, vivacious, popular. Now I was on a whole different plane of reality, characterized by self-loathing, pain, doubt, and angst. The whole edifice had begun to crumble—like in novels set at the twilight of the British Empire where there is always one lost soul—someone who is nervous, capable of fear, capable of doubt, capable of questioning—and this character presages the doom of the entire structure.

The emotion I experienced which set me apart from those in that class—the Curry Carters of the world—was doubt in myself. Much stronger, really: loathing of myself. If you cannot accept yourself, surely others will take the cue and cast you out—as you have cast yourself out. So confidence is one trait of that class. One of the tickets to admittance. The ability to dislike yourself and illuminate your craven nature could get you kicked out.

"He's sinking into a quagmire," said my mother.

But she thought everyone was sinking into a quagmire.

Other people's mothers sat at the kitchen table wearing a black lace slip drinking vodka in the middle of the day. Mine was on the field of battle with her sword drawn. It takes guts to be that person. That person stands amid the ruins and demands to know who is responsible. That person is not your pal, your buddy. That person is your mother: someone to wrangle with, to be stifled by, to escape from. But that person would pry me apart from fatuous boyfriends, detach me from drinking and drugs; she would point the way north that led to my salvation.

If this was a sacrifice, it of course escaped me at the time. The sacrifice your mother makes always escapes you at the time. In that way she confers your independence.

It really is quite apocalyptic to pine for your mother after she is gone but I wonder is it more apocalyptic to wish to protect her still.

She drove me home to my decaying apartment in the Garden District that day after lunch. While driving down the

Avenue she pointed out a funeral home that was being converted to a bookstore. Some people criticized it.

"At least it's not another liquor store," said my mother.

It was a funny thing coming from someone who drank three cocktails of brandy and ginger ale—"the drunkard's drink"—every night before dinner. And then took two Mickey Finns to get to sleep. But that was the funny thing about my mother. Her Radcliffe braininess and Yankee puritanism were hard to square with her own excesses.

Still she took up her weapons and renewed her attack.

"He's still young and already going downhill. He's been going downhill since I've known him."

"He's had a lot of tragedy in his life to contend with."

"He is a man who will one day crack—and that day may be soon. Don't kid yourself, my dear," she said.

"I admit that something in the man seems broken. The picture is askew."

"Hasn't it always been?"

There was a biblical downpour going on when I got home. There was a biblical downpour every day at certain times of the year. The month was September.

I received a visitor. The blue-eyed boy with the crooked smile. My mother's nemesis.

He was twenty-eight years old. So not really a boy, then. A

young man. There was something else. Something hell-bent. But something sublime. Kind of a Don Giovanni type of thing actually.

In his face it could be read that he had suffered losses. But to the casual observer this was disguised—as was the sublime hell—by his mild-mannered style and attire.

He had been in his share of scrapes. Earthquakes in California, every major hurricane that hit Louisiana, he had been run over by a car, struck by lightning, drowned—and had so far emerged, like me, miraculously unscathed.

Our fathers were old friends. Their outlook on life was similar. Wastrel youth was to them a season of life you were supposed to go through, and then that chapter would close. Though twenty-eight years old is a little late for youth. Maybe the pinnacle of youth. But downhill from there—as far as youth.

He was in a solitary and unusual line of work. He was an inventor. He had invented a shrimp-peeling machine when he was twenty-two that was in widespread use. He was working out a process of converting alcohol to gas that was at least a quarter century ahead of its time.

I saw in him a loping generosity and angelic self-effacement that dispelled my doubts in man. I kept missing the flip side. His angelic self-effacement was causing him to ruin his life. Or at least it dampened his will to fight patent infringements. One day a ruthless man of finance would get hold of the chance to manufacture and distribute these inventions. Talent is never enough for success. Self-effacement will lose the game early on.

Once I asked him what it's like to be an inventor. He said it's like sitting alone in your room all day watching your personality disintegrate. Similar to being a writer, he imagined.

But I guess we all had some sort of self-esteem problem.

A few days earlier he had a disturbing lunch with his father. That lunch also took place at the Pontchartrain—the preferred meeting place of one's parent. His father, a man with profusely wild white eyebrows and steel blue eyes, in a white linen suit, seemed frail.

He was in awe of his father. It was partly the leftover awe that a boy (as opposed to a man) has for his father. Access to your childhood is sharp when you live in the town you were born in. Once a year when he was a boy his father took him downtown to a hotel suite where the Brooks Brothers sales representative would set up the offerings and a man could have them ordered. On Sundays his father sometimes took him for a boat ride in the park and bought him Cracker Jacks. For his birthday his father took him to the Pontchartrain Hotel to have the baked Alaska. His father seemed to him like the most powerful man in America—a man who could negotiate incredibly complex and threatening things, like go to banks and get money and order suits of clothes.

We went to a bar in the Irish Channel. The dramatic rainstorm was still going on. The biblical deluge. Rain was coming down in buckets seemingly hurled against the windows. He told me my forehead had a noble mien. "Your forehead has a noble mien," he said.

He told me he had seen a vision of the Virgin Mary in the drugstore that day. He had seen a vision of the Virgin Mary once before—in the gym at school in sixth grade.

"You saw the Virgin Mary in the drugstore. What was she doing?" I asked.

"Just standing there."

"Did anyone else see her?"

"No, but she saw them."

Another item briefly mentioned somewhere in our conversation seemed to penetrate my consciousness. He had resigned from the Boston Club because they didn't take Jews. The angels were visiting Abraham, he said, and some strangers came in. Abraham kicked out the angels to welcome the strangers. That's what's great about Abraham, he explained.

"Don't you ever need time to just throw yourself across the bed and just start sobbing?" I responded.

"Girls do that a lot," he observed. "Men not so much."

I was preparing to deliver a speech on historic preservation that night for my job at the historic preservation society—I tried to save old buildings. I had a phobia of public speaking and tended to have breakdowns at the podium.

"Judy Garland was like that," he mused.

"Now there's something you don't hear every day. I'm like Judy Garland."

I rattled the ice cubes in my drink in the way Technique had taught me when I was a little kid. That was how you made a drink cold.

"Maybe I'm sinking into a quagmire," I suggested. "Maybe I should become more regular and not pursue vague dreams with no assurance of achieving the desired destination."

"But sweetheart, what else would you rather be doing?" he asked.

He had told me to treat my anxiety with gallantry. I wasn't sure what it meant. But it sounded promising. I would pretend that my anxiety was a distinguished visitor and treat it kindly with respect, make it sit down, tell it to keep calm—or tactfully pretend that it was normal. I wasn't sure.

We gallantly took our despair to the Alabama Gulf Coast. While we were there he was ungallantly struck by lightning. After almost being electrocuted our activities went on as before. There was a lurid glamor in the night.

The next day a certain evidence of fall was in the air—the Southern fall—a hot fall, amid the oaks, the kind that in childhood when you went home from school with a friend, their mother would be sitting at the kitchen counter wearing a black lace slip and drinking vodka, staring out at the velvet green lawns.

He picked up his motorcycle at my apartment and drove it

to his decaying apartment on Carondelet Street. He stopped at the bar on the corner. There was a collection of locals sitting at the bar—cops, old guys, regulars—he stopped to joke around with them. He was pretending to be a normal person and it was working, but suddenly he was stricken with feeling horrendously awful. Maybe it was from riding around in the excessive heat in the broad of day in the heavy black suit on the motorcycle.

Maybe it was from thinking of his father. He was concerned that his father had never really recovered from the death of a younger son. Claude's life had been defined by this too. He wanted to protect his father. Some lingering responsibility seemed to paralyze him.

The truth was that when he compared himself to his father—and his father was a man of quality, a man who had taken on his own father's burdens—he felt himself to be inferior. That's where the naked bulb shines. It may have been a small and seedy world, but if he saved his soul—like Rick in Casablanca—then he would always have that to live upon and steer his star by. That was what his father had.

When he got home he tried to drown out these anxieties with a recording of Winston Churchill's World War II speeches (We will fight them on the land, we will fight them on the sea, we will never surrender), which he thought would be fortifying. You would have heard them emanating from his decaying bungalow over and over on Saturday night.

In the evening he went to the barber on the corner of State and Magazine. The pace was slow at the barbershop. The pace of life was slow in general. The barber knew him. They joked around for a while. A cousin strolled in and took his seat in one of the four chairs situated in a row beneath the ceiling fans. They joked around some more.

August Anhalt came in on his way home from work. It was about six o'clock. He took a chair next to Claude.

Both wore the same clothes they seemed to have been wearing twenty years ago and so shared the same lack of vanity. But the youth with the sublime hell in his eyes lacked the stiff Germanic backbone that held the Anhalts to the straight and narrow.

"How's the old man?" said August Anhalt.

"The same as ever."

"Give him my regards."

But about an hour later as he was listening to Churchill intone his transmogrifying expressions of willpower on the tape he had brought home from London, in hopes it would transmogrify his own existence, he got the news about his father.

2.

This story does not start at the same old party. I would have to be the same old girl for that. And we would have to still be going to the same old parties. And that's the whole point. We are not. Maybe that is the romantic version. This one is illuminated by the naked bulb. Or at least partially naked.

The hero is one already well acquainted with grief, who knows what it's like to wake up in the morning facing his losses. Each loss is a diminishment and not alone a grief.

When your father drops dead in the prime of his life from a massive heart attack on the steps of Camellia Grill one evening in his seersucker suit, that is the pivotal moment that changes your life. The world turns on that moment. You come to a fork in the road.

There is a universe in which your father drops dead on the steps of Camellia Grill in his seersucker suit and although the event is unexpected, you are prepared to take up the gauntlet and step into his shoes and carry his burdens and meet his challenges for the rest of your life. There is a parallel universe in which the central event is the same but the reaction is different, and sets off a chain of unique calamities endemic to a world that had stayed the same for many generations. More by default than design, since the depressed economy, the closed society—these were the things that really perpetuated it.

For the previous generation it was different. Their aim was not escape. If offered positions elsewhere, they would decline. You took up your fathers' burdens.

Take the story of Ditto Perette. His father was a fifty-five-year-old man in a seersucker suit who had directed the family shipping company for thirty years. The boy left behind at his death—Ditto Perette—was a youth who possessed no knowledge of business. But suddenly there he was in a heartbreaking suit and tie going downtown every morning to deal with the ancient secretaries and the mysteries of the shipping business and run it straight into the ground by a mixture of innocence and an instinct for havoc and failure so spectacular that the shock still resounds.

That was the story of Ditto Perette, who had five sisters. It was in a place and time where the five sisters would not have been considered for the job. It would not have occurred to anyone—including the five sisters—that they might be interested in the job, or fitted for it. Despite the fact that anyone who thought Ditto would be suited for it did not process thought on a plane of rationality.

Trouble often tends to lie where it is not expected. Often it comes from within. There it is festering away in your own soul. Or in your father's business.

Collier & Grace was a storied law firm whose clients were such heavy hitters—the utilities, the Cotton Exchange, the Shipping Board—that there was no thought of seeking out new ones. No advertising, no rainmakers, no cold calls. Those practices were alien. It was not a part of the law that generation had been trained for.

But maybe the heavy-hitting clients were now thinking of decamping. Maybe some already had.

Many had fallen fast for the blue-eyed boy all his life. Some combination of sentiment and hope inspired the partners to ask the wayward scion to undertake the chief executive position then known as managing partner—he wouldn't practice law but his charisma would lure in clients and keep others from defecting.

In his heart Claude was shocked that the partners saw in him the potential to fulfill this role. In the crooked smile was a sympathy for all the hapless failure of the world; that was the theme of his character. They also missed the sublime hell—that was the other theme of his character.

One thing the partners did get right: he could not resist a call of distress.

In moments of sublime importance one sometimes fixates on a trivial thought. He would not have to obtain a new wardrobe to suit this novel role because although he worked at home and wallowed frequently in nothingness—from which he tried to create something—he didn't actually wear his bathrobe while doing it. He was the type of person who would wear a suit and tie to work at home. There was something curiously formal about him; his shirt would always be crisp; he would never look old.

There was his mother to think of. She had endured the worst that can be given: she had lost a son. In a way he felt she had recovered from it more than his father had. Women can be steely.

The true answer is more drab. You go where duty calls.

Or to put it another way: By George, let's get on with it.

So all put their hope in him.

All were mistaken.

All except Claire Anhalt, and even she could not have envisioned the magnitude of the disaster.

One lone voice tried to intervene. It came from my father. He was not accustomed to interfere in other peoples' lives. But he was compelled to address the young man as his old friend Louis Collier would have. And he knew exactly how he would have.

The meeting took place in the study of my father's house on a sweltering evening in October. As ever, the temperature in my father's house was freezing. Huge aspects of his life were focused on obstructing the tropic climate—travels to chilly Scottish fjords, enhanced generators to assure the operation of the AC in hurricanes.

He offered his visitor a cigar and they contemplated the oaks in the garden. A general conversation arose. This would break the ice. They discussed a mutual acquaintance.

"Some people don't like him, you know," said Claude.

"Most people don't like him," said August Anhalt.

"People say he's the salt of the earth."

"More like the pepper."

The ice was broken. They smoked their cigars.

"You don't have to do this, my boy."

There was a silence.

"This is not your bag," the older man went on.

A kind look was cast by the crooked smile, the sublime hell only slightly subdued.

"It happened to me," August Anhalt resumed, "but I loved the law; I also had a wife and a family on the way and a job waiting for me in New Orleans to support them. But you should get out while you can."

It looks like conformity to run the family firm, to live in the house you were born in. But these were practical decisions. From his children August Anhalt demanded independence.

He made no comment on the attachment of his daughter to the young man with the crooked smile. Someone else would deal with that, he knew.

"Follow your star, kid. Get out of this town, if that's where it leads." He stopped to let it sink in. He wasn't sure it did. "This is what your father would have wanted."

One of my brothers came upon my father sitting in the attic in his boxer shorts one day not long after that, staring into space. In some alarm my brother asked what he was doing. He said he was thinking about Louis Collier.

His old friend who had traversed the boulevards with him since they were boys. It was a harder loss for him than Curry Carter would be. Louis Collier was totally more my father's type of person. They studied ancient Greek together every

Wednesday night for forty years, taught by a Jesuit professor; and when the Jesuit professor died, they went on by themselves. The formal attire, the inexorable routine, the lifelong friendship through adversity.

In life I always wondered: Why wasn't I one of those diehard New Orleans people who would never leave? Like my father, but he was an unlikely one. That someone could be so antithetical to the reputed essence of New Orleans—revelry, etc.—yet so devoted to it seemed curious. We all know what was revelry for him. Ancient Greek, Latin fricatives, his book-lined house, its atmosphere of intellect and calm, an anchor in the storm.

I had a reverse anxiety about it, an exacerbated fear that I would be trapped there and unable to escape—by a storm, a hurricane, a flood. Which was certainly a possibility. And then what would I miss? The love of my husband and children—not wishing to retread the long and broken road that had led to them. There is always that mystery when you are young—the future. And now the future is the past.

Maybe it was hard on him that I soon moved away. It was too dangerous there. Too dangerous for some. Too dangerous for me. Storm Durant got on a train to Boston one day and never came back. She met a boy in a bar on the night of her arrival and married him shortly after. She provided him with a number of children and a fair amount of heartaches despite a complete reformation of her wild ways, and she would not be sitting at the kitchen table in a black lace slip drinking vodka when her kids came home from school. Gin Allstrom blew out of town on a midnight flight after falling off a balcony at a party and almost breaking his back, his suitcase packed with starched white pants from Louisiana, his hopes turned to the North. Each had his narrow escape.

But some things never change.

3.

How are the girls? People would ask when my daughters left for college.

"We're great except for our tendency to drive into inanimate objects," said Adelaide. She had collided with a defunct bus stop in Kalorama the week after she got her license by driving directly into it and smashing it to bits. Thank the Lord it was defunct. Adelaide was unharmed. Only the bus stop was wiped off the face of the earth. For years we kept seeing a dull mound of earth surrounded by scaffolding at a sharp turn in Connecticut Avenue where it once had been.

After Grace got her license she drove—albeit somewhat daintily—into a brick wall. She too emerged unscathed. The brick wall was also spared.

"Maybe it was the other guy's fault," people said.

"I don't think so considering the other guy was a brick wall."

They had wild parties when Jack and I were out of town, they took midnight boating trips in Georgetown, they stole their father's gin. I was weirdly mellow about it. Probably because of my expertise on wastrel youth.

The towering mid-Atlantic spring had come and gone. It was early June. I was reading a book about nuns. Normally I wouldn't read a book about nuns in fourteenth-century Flanders, but since I was forced to, I found it surprisingly interesting. It was one of my duties as an adjunct professor in Baltimore to judge a fiction prize of first novels for the university's press. The one about nuns was my favorite. Probably I like reading about nuns because I wasn't taught by nuns. People who were taught by nuns find them scary and repressive and weird.

No one ever said that Catholics don't have aspects of being boring, though. Take Nancy Pelosi. No one ever thought of Nancy Pelosi as a deep intellectual thinker. It's more that she's a force of nature. Eighty-two years old, her hair is gorgeous, she's never not in high heels, dressed to kill, while briskly covering vast distances along the tunnels of the Capitol, where she ruled 600 men with an iron pragmatism.

But dressed to kill, like ladies from another generation. Amelia was like that too. So were the ladies at Grand Hotel on the Alabama coast.

Where my old flame—a Catholic who would have preferred to be Jewish, a pretty rare type, but far more rare in that part of the world—gallantly took his despair.

I heard in time over the years that he was married and had three or more children. His father's will conferred on him substantial benefits. He dispossessed himself of them. But dispossession is too mild a word. Volcanic destruction would be better.

For ninety years the law firm of Collier & Grace had occupied dim corridors on two floors of the Louisiana Bank Building, where threadbare Oriental runners lined the halls and quaint hand-painted arrows pointed your direction on frosted-glass doors along the corridors. The marts of commerce seemed very distant from this atmosphere. There was a judicious purpose in the threadbare modesty. The overhead was low.

Claude moved the firm to one of the sleek new skyscrapers then being built downtown. It was thought the change of quarters would represent an effort to step up to the plate and progress to the future, to catch up with Atlanta or Houston, and not stay mired in the past.

But the clients defected anyway, the real estate market collapsed, and failure was ordained.

Maybe it was the nature of the place. Or the nature of the world.

At some point a girl comes to realize the knowledge that men go to brothels; maybe a girl comes to realize this sooner in a town like New Orleans where at age seven she accidentally sees strippers while walking down the street. Bourbon Street, that is—holding the hand of her mother taking the child to her ballet class. Strippers and sleaze, integral to the hometown, it is observed in childhood. It is reasonable to assume they are integral to life in general. To conclude that not all men watch strippers at three p.m. or go to prostitutes but some men do, or else there would not be strippers and prostitutes in the world.

Claude was the type of man who did. I had always heard about it. He went to brothels and/or Bourbon Street sex professionals. But did this faze me? No. Some men are like that or there would not be brothels in the world.

He was a big man physically. You could get lost in his arms. One night after his father's sudden death before I moved away, I had a shock to see him standing naked in the doorway of his father's mansion at midnight as I came up the path. There was something chilling yet sublime about it. About him. An infernal ravishment. There was a naked man silhouetted in the night—but a man who went to brothels and/or weird sex professionals—what could draw you to make the act of love with such a man?

His soul—there was a big soul—with him you felt his soul—it was a communication.

And how had such a worldly and forbearing girl, who always forgave him so easily his excesses, devolved into someone wearing a shroud and carrying a sign that said REPENT?

This is a question age asks looking back on her younger self.

*

A year later he was having drinks with some associates from work. Mojitos at a Cuban restaurant. It was All Saints' Day. When he got up from the table the room was spinning. He lurched through the parking lot—like James Bond after his martini has been poisoned in *Casino Royale*—till he came to the hotel across the street, a Hampton Inn on St. Charles Ave.

His demeanor at the reception desk the next morning when he checked out was that of an eighth-grade boy on the debate team: sheer panic and total composure all at the same time.

He went into the bookstore next door. He stood before a giant coffee-table art book entitled *Flemish Primitives*. He studied it in a trance. An epiphany occurred. He would go to Ghent. Or was it Brussels. Anywhere they had Flemish primitives would do. The idea was Vermeer. To spend your entire life in one room saying: let's break it down—this one room—this corner of this one room.

The clients were defecting in mass droves, the partners had held secret meetings to depart for greener pastures, the accounts were dwindling and the books unbalanced.

"Take a step back," he told himself. "Look at the big picture."

That's what really scared him.

*

He drove down to Araby, as in The Sheik of. Then down to Violet. On the way back the usual biblical deluge happened. He would have to wear his father's gigantic duck-hunting boots to wade through the streets and pick up dinner. Luckily they were in the trunk of the car. The trunk of his car always contained duck-hunting boots, an ice chest, and a basketball. Items that might or might not come in handy, but they were always there.

He went to the Lebanese café on Carrollton. There were resounding claps of thunder that sounded more like gunshots. Then he headed down St. Charles to the Quarter. It was raining, it was humid, it was decaying, it was hot, the Quarter was filled with tourists schlepping along haplessly trying to pretend they were having a good time. He pushed through the traffic and turned off at Elysian Fields to go back by the river where it was quiet and then he felt better, much better, in the peace and quietude and green along the levee.

On the way uptown he took a better route—St. Claude—where there was no traffic and the decaying houses were somehow less oppressive, maybe because the general decay was even more at an extreme, and the extreme had somehow purified the angst. Or maybe it was the lack of hapless tourists in their hideous outfits pretending to have a good time at depressing Planet Hollywood franchises, etc.—nothing could be more depressing than that.

For dinner he went to the Pontchartrain. The waitresses

were gazing at him pensively. Soon they were gazing at him adoringly.

The Pontchartrain was in decline. How the deserted restaurant stayed open one doesn't know. But it was where he had last seen his father—and for that reason he tended to frequent the place. He might not have put it to himself that way. But there was no other explanation for it really, unless to palliate the matter in some communion with his father.

Although he was only twenty-nine he seemed like someone who had passed beyond the stage of youth and was just trying to get through something—some form of pain, both mental and physical.

But this did not repel the waitresses from their fascination with him; perhaps it increased their fascination. His tragic air seemed to galvanize their interest. Somehow the general public saw their own redemption, the hope that they themselves had lost, in him. They saw a tall man with a curious self-effacement dripping with glamour in his seersucker suit there at the ends of the earth.

4.

My mother did not have what's called the gift of faith, but she did say this much in our last conversation. "I'm not going to die. I'm going to live. There is a little girl with blond curls and green eyes"—my last daughter, Grace—"I'm going to live in her."

A tall man with an air of solitude wearing baggy khaki pants and a pale yellow shirt came to visit us a few days after my mother's funeral. He meandered up the path somewhat abstractedly. It was striking because most people come to pay their respects to the family after a funeral all together in a drove and perhaps most don't have the courage or heart to wait a while and stalk forth alone like he did.

He was kind of the strong silent type, and he appeared to have nothing in particular to say, but obviously wanted to offer his support and let us know how he felt about Claire Anhalt. Maybe the awkwardness came from the fact that we all knew how Claire Anhalt had felt about him.

At this time the Collier Distiller and the shrimp-peeling machine, inventions of his youth whose ironclad patents were protected by the legal machinations of his late father, were in widespread use, providing the support of his dependents. We chatted about his life. Louise was renovating the kitchen. It was causing a crisis. She thought the tiles looked pink.

"But she thinks everything looks pink," he said.

We looked outside to the garden and palm trees. It was 95 degrees, being July, and you could see the heat rising up from the pavement in mists.

He seemed to be struggling to deliver a message. Finally he came up with it.

Do not trust in yourself until the day you die, he quoted from the bible. He said it was from the Torah. There is this belief that however devout you may be, he went on, some error may still be committed very late in life. God took your mother before her time so she could go to her reward before she sinned and was forbidden that reward.

It was a funny thing coming from him. This was a man who had Bourbon Street sex professionals in his life. And communicated with the Virgin Mary.

After an interval he shook hands with my father.

"My best to you always, my boy," said my father, and we watched him walk off down the Avenue under the grandiose oaks.

Some years later I went back to Grand Hotel with Jack. The hotel on the Alabama coast. There was beauty everywhere in the small Southern town on the bay.

Everyone seemed inordinately happy. The women had blond hair and cheerful polite demeanors, and were droll. They had certain layers of complexity that I was not entirely sure I could successfully navigate. The I-don't-take-any-of-your-guff layer. The no-nonsense get-it-done layer. The layer of: Yes, I wear heavy necklaces that match my varying outfits even if I'm wearing shorts, and my hair is immaculately coiffed and groomed. But make no mistake: I'm witty and I'm tough and I don't take any of your guff.

I saw my old flame after dinner—though I would not have thought it was the type of place that he would go to now. Years ago I was there with him when he got struck by lightning and emerged unscathed.

He was gripping the handles of a wheelchair containing a small towheaded boy that he was steering along the bay, stopping to look at various birds and crabs skittering down the shore. It was one of those situations that you might assume to be painful and tortured and pathetically sad. But it was obviously not. A sublime love was evident in the face of both father and son.

He was about forty years old then. I had often asked myself why there was no other woman after his wife—the long-suffering Louise. His love affairs had always been numerous. In addition to the Bourbon Street–style sex professionals. Maybe they still were in his life. Mysterious bad influences, maybe drug related, rough contacts. There was somehow his marriage in the midst of all that, and a baby born too soon, with handicaps.

More children were born, and at some point, Louise decamped. When she left she took the children—except for the handicapped son. Claude lived alone with the handicapped boy and raised him and saw to his needs. Shocking that Louise would have left it that way but apparently she could not handle the extra demands of the handicap—and that was one among various that he could. Or she knew that he would. It was what he was suited for.

Maybe that is the difference between the devoted and the detached, the die-hard and the escaper.

The next night we ran into him at dinner. He hated the buffet. "Why are there so many priests here?" he kept asking. We ran into a priest who had been one of his teachers at the Catholic school he attended as a boy.

"What was he like as a child?" I asked the priest.

"He was all right," said the priest.

"Not exactly ringing praise," said Claude.

"I thought you quit smoking," I said.

"I only smoke when I drink."

"I thought you quit drinking."

"I only drink on Fridays. And the weekends..."

I had just quit smoking and told him it was giving me trouble with writing—I couldn't write without smoking.

"Carlyle could only write with his head leaning against a cold mantel," he said helpfully.

5.

His boyhood habitat was in the swamps across the lake. Bayou Chinchuba runs parallel to Lake Pontchartrain from Lewisburg to the Tchefuncte River in Madisonville. There was nothing closer to his heart than the bald-cypress swamp of the

Chinchuba. Snakes, frogs, critters, bugs, he knew all about them. Went around in a pirogue checking his traps like a Cajun.

The weather on the Chinchuba would to me be suffocating but it was first in his heart—a far cry from the Atlantic surf where I go now. If he ever came there he would wait till fall when all the people had left, and go alone at five a.m. to the Atlantic in his waders.

"What does a man think about when he goes fishing?" I asked him once.

"Not small matters."

It is surprising how much you can love someone. One does not often feel such love. It has to do with New Orleans of course. But there is more to it. Something to do with my long-held love for my dear friend, his forbearing wife, Louise. Not that Miss Spiritual Exercises of St. Ignatius over here would ever do anything untoward. But that there is some sort of tortured quality to my love for him. It's hard to put my finger on it.

He had many trials, and had them for years, decades; I was almost surprised that he was still around, considering. I worried about him from time to time, probably in visions in the night when God speaks.

Could have sworn I saw him at dinner in the restaurant at the Ace in Brooklyn the other night. Kept thinking I would run into him or thinking everyone was him. I looked up to him. People I look up to don't grow on trees.

*

I was beginning to think he was a figment of my imagination, as I didn't see him again until ten years later. It was at a plantation in the Louisiana countryside called Perseverance. A branch of his family had lived there since the Civil War and farmed the land. Sugarcane was doomed but they had more luck with soybeans. They had names like Po-boy and Peanut and took their vacations at a summer house in the next town one mile away.

To get there you went through the swamps outside of New Orleans towards Baton Rouge and took the ferry at Gramercy across the Mississippi River, then followed the levee the rest of the way. It was pretty much at the ends of the earth.

My father used to take us there for parties and reunions. Recently I watched a video of the place that was made in 1965—and there I saw the ghosts in their remote nether realm. Alice Anhalt, vibrant and flirtatious in old age, the star of the show, giving droll brusque toasts, stately as a white-haired admiral speaking in Parliament. Louis Collier—God what a great-looking guy—rugged, dark, in his seersucker suit and bow tie and horn-rims—with a spark. And there was the blue-eyed boy with the crooked smile and the sublime hell in his soul. And there was I myself, toddling about at the beginning of life, among the ghosts in their now remote nether realm.

"They must have let the angels out of heaven," he said when he saw me.

It was extremely odd that he had retreated there—it must have been out of necessity. Two more of his inventions, which comprised unusual discoveries in navigation, were being put in use on ocean-going vessels; the proceeds continued to support his dependents.

While he retreated to a dysfunctional Perseverance.

"I raised that little scamp there," said a black man walking past, nodding at the portly fifty-year-old Claude.

"Did he raise you?" I asked when the man walked on.

"*No!* He just says that. He saw me around."

"You think he's handsome now?" said the man walking past again. "You should have seen him forty years ago."

"You got that right," I said.

We were making him squirm.

"You're so interesting," I said lamely to break the ice.

"I haven't said anything interesting since 1999," he said cheerfully.

"Very funny." I looked away. "You just said something interesting."

For a while he had a job driving the courtesy van at a Toyota dealership in Shreveport. For a while he was a chauffeur in Texas. He was like the scientist whose research was the indispensable piece that caused the others to get the Nobel Prize and when the newspapers found him in some obscure location driving the courtesy van at a Toyota dealership to ask him how he felt about it, he calmly said they had devoted their lives to science whereas he had worked sporadically.

"I know, you think I'm Gloria Swanson in *Sunset Boulevard*," he said.

There was a book on his desk. It was called *Time, Love, Memory*.

"How fascinating," I commented.

"Yes but not really," he said. "It's only about fruit flies."

I looked at it later. It described experiments with fruit flies, but you could draw analogies to humans. In one experiment, when the scientist did something that made the fruit flies happy, they started doing a conga line. If the scientist kept giving them the happiness thing, they literally did the conga line on the way to their death.

We walked around the grounds. "I haven't spoken to Louise in a year," he said mildly. "And my boy has gone to college in the North," he said with pride. So for his son he paved the way—escape velocity.

I remember when I was seventeen years old sitting in my room at home and this strange sensation came over me, as if I could see down the broken road and knew that it would lead—out of town. Leaving for college, a sensation of peace, finally going out into the world—delayed by a hurricane, of course.

"So how are you, really?" he asked me.

"I have a gnawing sense of anxiety in the pit of my stomach—but as you taught me—who doesn't?"

Which is a huge relief to realize.

He looked at me sideways, with those dazzling blue eyes.

You would speak of his graceful hands, his tall upright frame—not of decrepitude, reeking of alcohol, for somehow those did not stand out. There was something curiously formal about him; his shirt would always be crisp; he would never look old. It was a comfort to think that I could always go and see him, along that backward route, inescapable from all directions, on the broken road that leads back home.

There were two bridges spanning the Mississippi River in New Orleans. People used to commit suicide there. One was the high society bridge for suicide. The other was the egalitarian choice. In Washington there were statistics in suicide about who chose the Duke Ellington Bridge compared to those who chose the Taft. In New Orleans you would always hear stories about some society woman, the mother of children, who would make her way up to the top of the Mississippi River Bridge and plummet to what would have to be the most frightening way possible in which to meet your doom. Which would not only take daring, gall, and depression. There were less frightening ways to commit suicide. It would have to be a product of insanity.

He could have done that. In a way it would fit his quest for destruction.

I heard what happened to him in Katrina. There was a welter of chaos. His mother had not evacuated. What aged mother with infirmities or grandmother of eighty could bear it? The dashing escapes. The tedious exits. The unendurable traffic and waits at the restroom, etc. His mother had moved to a small apartment and had some trouble with her bills. But he did still try to protect her, and lived with her there for a time.

When it was too late after the storm and she was sinking he could not get her out. She died, and he had to arrange a funeral in Texas as it was impossible to have one in New Orleans. He literally had to bring his mother to her own funeral. He had a pistol; there were starving people along the roads on the way out. When it was all over he caught a plane in Dallas back to New Orleans. He realized that he still had the pistol and gave it to the taxi driver.

A year after Katrina I stayed at the Pontchartrain, which had developed an odd air of corruption since the storm. Maybe even before, I don't know. The oaks and foliage were still sick and sparse, some telephone poles leaning as if they were about to crash down. The Pontchartrain had an air of despair. My room was next to the Ethel Merman suite. The Carol Channing suite was down the hall. You could easily connect those people with the place in its heyday—there's no business like show business, cocktails, cigarettes, cigars and baked Alaska.

I felt a crushing unease, and recalled the memorable lunch I had there with my mother, when she somehow propelled me from that world into a wider one. If you were a genius you could see the universe in one small town. But I could not. And while I was pondering these things at the Pontchartrain I received a call from Gin Allstrom to inform me that Claude Collier had died of a heart attack, at a much younger age than that of his father before him.

The mind is not shocked but the heart cannot accept the information.

Later it was said he seemed to know the end was near. Few would admit that he could have been glad the end was near. But then who could be glad of the end being near, save the most inordinate sufferer, and few would admit that Claude was really that. But it would be like him to be that and not let on. The angelic self-effacement.

No one can know if he suffered, or how much, because he kept it to himself if he did. An intricate process of objective scientific study conducted inwardly on his hell-bent soul.

Sometimes in life I find myself standing in the middle of a room repeating his name when ridden with angst and anxiety, trying to calm down. I don't know exactly why. But to this day when I am nervous and mired in angst and malaise, I still say his name.

> Even when he was a young man everything about him had promised disaster...
>
> —Alice Roosevelt

Opera, Oysters, the World

My father's study looked like a cross between the laboratory of a mad scientist and a repository of documents in a Kafka novel after a tornado. He did not come from a generation whose correspondence was stored electronically. He was reliant on random kind souls who sometimes materialized to help with his filing. Amelia and the nurses drew the line at filing.

A random kind soul materialized—me. I felt that we shared the DNA of needing to be organized with Germanic precision, so I alphabetized the files. Or made a start on it. I wished I could alphabetize more of the files, but there were too many: The Meaning of Life, The Decadence of Society, Yugoslavian Visions, Annoyances and Frustrations, Eccentric Commercial Practices, Byzantine Patriarchs, Purgatory, Greek Macros, Latin Fricatives, etc.—and the enigmatic "Too Hard" file.

I suggested we lose the Laments file and put its meager two-page contents in a Miscellaneous file. His quite enthusiastic acceptance of the Miscellaneous file—my proud creation, to deal with all the extra papers everywhere—I took as a token of his love. But as to losing the Laments file he said, Never—because if you need a lament you need it right away.

Amelia had some anxiety about visitors and the length of their visits. Visitors were allowed to stay for one hour, but I made my own exception. I was assertive. And it was all because of the filing. That was the only way I could engage with him, at this point, I told her. I guess she did not know that till I said it. The whole thing about her maybe not knowing my viewpoints because I don't say them. I know who I am, why don't you? Oh yeah, because I hid what I felt.

When I bid her goodbye, I shed a tear, though I do not know if she noticed.

Louise would rage if it were near the end and I was not welcomed to be there. But after all, my upbringing raised me to be stoic. And all he did for me lived on within: abstractions and ideals, his legacies intangible and ingrained. Louise was on the warpath anyway—the funerals, the drunks, the parties, it was getting to her.

A few weeks later my dear father was in the hospital again with pneumonia, the usual round of Mardi Gras parades halting progress of the ambulance and making it dicey for Amelia to visit him.

My dear father died that day.

I was thinking of the time we went to Monticello, and saw Jefferson's diary that recounts: "On this day my dear wife died."

The exhibition hinted that he wallowed in his grief. On closer examination the passage in a meticulous small hand was not as romantic as had been suggested:

I lent $45 to Mr. Rivers. Sold a cow. Got bacon. My dear wife died.

But I get that now. The pain is in the restraint.

Finding out you're an idiot is not a totally pleasant experience, but your ability to discern that you're an idiot is a promising sign. Weddings and funerals bring out the worst in people, I've heard it said. I knew everyone was annoying before, so why should I be surprised that they are annoying now? Because you don't expect to be annoyed in bereavement. You expect to be bereaved.

Whereas harping on the people who bug you—why? It's the wrath again. Why does it have to be wrath as well as sorrow. The garden of wrath blooming away, even at such a time. Such ills should be banished. Deposed and banished like the kings in Shakespeare.

According to Amelia you can't have a funeral during Mardi Gras—the weeks leading up to it—because everyone has to go to Mardi Gras related luncheons. I don't know who these people are who have those priorities. Others have to go on their vacations to the Caribbean. So a memorial service was scheduled for some few weeks hence. I thought you were supposed to cancel your vacations and Mardi Gras luncheons for a funeral when your dear father dies. But these are the customs of the place, of the die-hard inhabitant. The inexorable revels that comprise the personality of the town.

So I would go back to Washington and return for the memorial service. I asked Amelia if I should stay to help in any way I could and offered my support. It was declined.

Prediction error: when we expect one thing and find another, that defies our expectations. The curtain rises, like the opening of an opera, or a veil removed that had obscured the scene, whose meaning now could be revealed. I had always planned to help Amelia when this time came, having retained but perhaps miscalculated the nature of our friendship. Her reality was that I was a stepping stone whose friendship she would always remember and doubtless treasure in some way. Some sentimental way of remembrance and gratitude. For me it was not relegated to the realm of memory. It was still a living fact. I wonder if that is always the way in this situation. That it's dicey when your friend marries your father.

It's poignant that I'm so dense/clueless but that's not even exactly the most poignant part. The poignant part is having gotten it wrong. Having not got the message, till now.

If you happened to have a little thing called a brain, you would have gotten it long before, and also known that in the magnitude of her bereavement, there was no room to share her grief.

There was a beautiful view from my room of oaks and the long-since-replaced broken-down magnolia tree—now a madly blooming one. It was strangely mesmerizing. Considering it's just trees.

And I don't know what Greek macros are, and I thought I didn't care about them, but while looking at a sizable file about them later in the overflowing library, something swept over me and I decided to keep it.

Soon the untoward wrath returned. My brothers annoyed me—mansplaining, pontificating, their words received with awe by others—and I had wrath instead of sorrow.

We went to the cemetery to do business and paperwork. How well I remembered seeing him bury my mother there when I saw his place flagged at the site. For the image of your father standing at your mother's grave bidding her goodbye is not one that can fade from your soul.

In a volume of Thucydides in his library I found that night there was a funeral oration. He had underlined one passage in it, a truth I see I must have learned from him: "For it is not by receiving kindness, but by conferring it, that we acquire our friends."

There is a theory that the world is divided into two kinds of people: continuers and dividers. The continuers can tell they are the same person they always used to be; the dividers repeatedly change. Music, the gift bequeathed by my father, led me to make the distinction.

It started with Bach. The atmosphere of Bach is stern and steadfast and uncompromising. Some people are too emotional about it when playing Bach. You might even say sappy. Emotion in Bach is the result of bracing discipline, firm and upright. Not upright as in morally upright, just straight—a straight shooter, a straight arrow. An inexorable bass line unwaveringly braces the foundation. It can never be broken.

This does convey an emotion, and that emotion is JOY. Joy is a more stern form of happiness.

In Venice with my father when Grace was twelve he took us to approximately one zillion churches to look at the Carpaccios. He pointed out the red bird in the corner of a Carpaccio he said had led him to have an epiphany in 1958. Every day his secretary FedEx-ed him hard copies of the New Orleans *Times-Picayune*, which he read on the boats while gliding past the palazzos with their marble angels, the ornate architecture everywhere, sometimes opera playing, on the green canals. We had oysters on an ancient court with Moorish arches and white umbrellas under awnings crisply flapping in the wind.

Opera, oysters, the world.

He took us to a cathedral in the Adriatic lagoon that showed the green of Paradise, the legions of the blessed, and the angels unfurling the starry sky of night to the end of time. He called it the Last Judgment.

But that's only the tip of the iceberg. I can't keep up with my father while traveling. No one could. After going to six zillion churches, sometimes we had to go back to the same church to see something we had missed or mistaken—like we looked at the wrong altarpiece, or missed the picture of God.

"Mom, do you think I'm capable of fully appreciating all the beauty I'm seeing, at my age?" Grace asked me one day amid all the frescoes and old masters.

"Maybe not."

She seemed relieved.

I was always captivated by the dueling orchestras at the Florian and the Quadri in the square. It must have been the off-season as there were no crowds. The waiters in white-tie and tails paced about the deserted arcade with its billowing white curtains in the ancient arches, the vast old square lit up, as the orchestras played on gallantly without an audience.

My father left his cigars to Jack. Amelia thought they were ruined, moldering away in the basement, since he hadn't smoked them in three years or taken care of them. Jack went down to check and they were all perfectly magnificent, he found. It turns out cigars are not like wine. Cigars want heat and humidity. Jack was overjoyed.

Then there was his will. It was beautiful—and awkward—to see his handsome gesture towards me and my brothers. It meant a lot to me though I felt guilty, considering. Considering how much Amelia and her daughters had done for him in the last twenty-three years. Considering that they had done everything and we had done nothing.

When a man dies, his lawyer reads his will and distributes it to his heirs. Resentments, surprises, shocks can ensue. I claim no stake in the outcome because I am not materialistic. But mostly because I am married to a tycoon. I have no quibble as to where the chips may fall. I only see who needs the chips.

He knew I didn't need the chips, but in Louisiana there is a thing called *usufruct*—leftover from the Napoleonic Code still used there, to which he was devoted. He also strongly advocated something called Forced Heirship. So you can see which way the wind is blowing on this. Usufruct can cut both ways, though. It confers the "temporary" right to derive income and benefit from an estate which ultimately reverts to the heir.

Our mild-mannered lawyer, Andrew Mallory, the executor of my father's estate, took me to lunch. He's the last living relic from Collier & Grace—Claude's father's law firm. He was asking me about Amelia. I explained the mutual devotion and love between her and my father and how much she had done for him.

"She's fierce," I added.

"Sacred Heart girls are always fierce," he said.

My father's estate is in some disorder. I think it might be something of a shock to some. He lived handsomely and was extremely generous, dispensing his largesse with a free hand. He seems to have been one who lived to the limit of his means. Not exceeding his means. But kind of to the outermost limits of them, especially during the last four years. It may not be exactly what I think everyone was expecting.

2.

During this time my father-in-the-law was in the hospital in treatment for an illness, but I saw his irrepressible nature and immunity to melancholy as a barrier to disease. As if to prove my theory, he was in a great mood. Never has one man had so much fun in a hospital. He was in a new wing. He loved it. He loved the nurses. He loved everything about it.

Then he took a sudden turn downhill. His doctor delivered some surprisingly bad news in a blunt manner. Dr. Doom, my father-in-law nicknamed the doctor with the bad bedside manner and bad news.

To say that my own father bore his diminishments with stoic dignity for the three years of his illness was kind of an understatement. I did not think my father-in-law would want to put up with it. The writing was on the wall at that point. My father-in-law wanted out. He made his wishes known to Stella, who was in charge of him. He told the nurses.

Soon he was mad at hospice because he thought it would be over sooner. What am I paying you for, etc. He started calling the pallbearers to line them up.

Dad they're not bridesmaids, said Jack.

But I feel like a bridegroom before the wedding, he said, near the end. A little nervous.

He died on Stella's birthday. We were there. He wanted to see us.

There was not much to see. Jack and I went out to dinner the night he died but Stella refused to leave her father's side.

Some things you can't forget. After it was over and the heroic hospice nurses do the mysterious things they heroically do then, the funeral home is called and thirty minutes after that two strapping tall elegant North Carolina black men in a hearse arrive in the night to wheel him out in a body bag, delivering stalwart words of comfort and condolence as they depart.

At first it is exhilarating to see it all like the curtain rising and then closing on a stage but later these same images are haunting. My father-in-law's end seemed benign at first but from the next day onward it seemed violent.

Also it seemed gallant. He was doing for Stella what he could not fully do for her in life. Confer her independence. He hastened to his end, maybe that's all part of the gallantry and the violence. What his daughter did for him in turn and the heroic way in which she did it over the months when he was in her care is something I can never forget.

But some images are haunting. Such as seeing him wheeled out in a body bag at midnight by the two strapping elegant black guys and having seen him at the end, this magnetic man who had such vitality. Who was ageless until three months ago. Something about his end wrenches your heart. His droll character and brave hurtle toward death.

What I do not understand—then or now—is why his death raised the direct grief that my own father's did not. I put it down to my devotion to abstractions, my claim of that immutability.

I just go from funeral to funeral giving orations.

Within me grief hath kept a tedious fast.

I left the day after my father-in-law's funeral at the crack of dawn for my rescheduled duties in New Orleans, engulfed in sorrow—to go through my father's papers and files. When I got there I was too busy to repine. Packing twenty-six boxes of his books and papers to send to relevant recipients and/or back to Washington, and digitizing an immense amount of photographs starting with his service in the army overseas in World War II. Seeing him as a soldier in these photographs you think: He belongs to the universe now—to the ages, the galaxies, etc.

And if even a god like that could kick the bucket, my turn is next.

The gift of faith—where is it now?

Then the job was done and the fathers in the ground and I collapsed. Maybe abstractions are not so great after all.

All the stuff I kept telling myself about how my father loved me, I revered him, he gave me all those abstract things that would endure to the end of time, so the intensity of my grief and shock was muted—when I went through his papers and was hit by a far worse grief than at his death I realized: I am going to be one of those people who can't grieve at the time so they have to have a giant breakdown later.

Stella said a raven came to the porch—she thought it might be her father. Nevermore, she called out to it.

Later when a raven crashed into my window twice—as if to get my attention, for it wasn't hurt and then perched on a nearby branch trying to look innocent—I realized that my father was communicating *through* Stella's father, who that night sent me a message from him during a streaming show. Hank Azaria was playing a Dick Van Dyke–type character from the 1950s. The scene shifted to black-and-white in honor of the era. After dinner he went to the piano with his cocktail and played a jazz song. His daughter had just gone on her first date and he had interviewed the young man who came to pick her up, and then was melancholy as he wandered over to the piano. His clothes, his manner, the jazzy song—it was all my father-in-law. But the sentiment was from my father. "My heart belongs to Delery," he sang at the piano with his cocktail. "My

Delery lights up the room when she walks in, and makes the world seem right," he crooned—more Nat King Cole than *Don Giovanni*—but equally ecstatic, as a light was cast on the stage and the curtain rose and there was everything—OPERA, OYSTERS, THE WORLD.

Lions And Daughters

MY DESCENT FROM HIGH SOCIETY is now complete. Being as my father was my entree to it. Not being August Anhalt's daughter is a gigantic comedown. At least when I'm in New Orleans. To step so effortlessly into the vanished world, where the curtain rises and the dramas multiply. And yet at every turn to suffer from remorse.

It's a problem. It's a serious problem.

Sometimes I feel like I'm beating a dead horse with the remorse. Like why did I have remorse, in my saga with Jack. Maybe because when you blame yourself, you're not the victim.

On the back flyleaf of my father's edition of *The Odyssey* is one of his cryptic notes: "Penelope's nightingale, p. 256." No further elaboration was given. So I made my own interpretation. By your sorrows you may be unbroken, but you will always return to them from time to time, wandering amid the ruins.

The lions snarling at the gate who thwart your purposes and bar your entrance from the desired realm, are they the ills within you? I would soon find out. Soon I met them in person, these lions snarling at the gate, and learned about them at first hand.

It was Jack's dream to go on an African safari. This was his long-held dream. So I would have the chance to observe these obtruding lions. And determine the source of their dominance. Unafraid and unrepentant—like Don Giovanni—is that their secret? Confidence, in a word. Not only courage.

The dream safari was postponed twice over two years for COVID. Finally we embarked on his dream safari. I had some doubts about the dream safari. I had just had hip-replacement surgery. These things wear out—your bones. Jack wanted me to do it so I'd be OK for his beloved African safari.

Certain other doubts arose about the dream safari. My daughters had political objections. "I don't want to have a butler in Africa," said Adelaide. A butler? That it would be luxury while everyone else was starving. Their father argued that the safari business supported jobs and the economy. Secretly I knew luxury wouldn't be the problem, really. How luxurious could it really be, in the middle of an endless desert or swamp or jungle in the middle of nowhere?

The problem would be wild animals. Not sure they'll want me hanging around.

Including lions. Snarling at the gate.

September 5, 2023

Emirates flight to Dubai; passengers predominately Indian and Arab. Watched some Middle Eastern TV shows just to see what they were like. They were moronic melodramas. Bar in back of plane with prayer times listed on TV screens—conflicting message? (Aren't Muslims not allowed to drink?)

Changed planes in Dubai for eight-hour flight to Johannesburg.

Landed at Johannesburg. The weather in Johannesburg ecstatic. Like California with the big sky and glittering clear air but warm like New Orleans. I always knew Africa would remind me of New Orleans. And that it would seem familiar for that reason. Like being in the cradle. Whether of civilization/humanity, or in the exact resemblance to the overwhelming black population of my childhood and youth there, not sure. My daughters would say I should explore, study, and unlearn certain aspects of these sentiments.

September 7, 2023

Flew to Zimbabwe, small plane, bumpy ride. We met our guide who took us directly to Victoria Falls. I was reading a biography of Livingstone, who supposedly discovered it in 1855 while searching for the source of the Nile. It's one endless series of disasters marching through swamps and jungles with killer ants devouring them in their tents or swarms of spiders covering them at night and getting malaria, dysentery, cerebral parasites, etc.

You can't describe Victoria Falls—it's too intense. Mainly you keep picturing those old movies where the people are innocently paddling down a placid river till too late they realize they're about to tip over a ten-thousand-foot waterfall...

Our guide took us to our first safari camp, on the Zambezi River. The staff is lined up waving at you when you arrive, like Downton Abbey. They told us all the rules. You're not allowed to walk around the grounds alone and must always be alert/aware. I had the feeling that my days were numbered. What about snakes? In the movies people who have lived in Africa their entire lives and love snakes get bitten by them and if you don't have the antidote at hand, it's all over. I asked them if they had the antidote at hand. They don't.

It was five o'clock. They drove us to the river in a jeep. One guide sits on a jump seat that is unfolded far out in front of the vehicle and very high above it. He must be very brave as it does not seem safe. He is the tracker. When you set off he is looking all around intently—like the Indian trackers in James Fenimore Cooper—and has eyes which can see great distances like human binoculars.

Two minutes after we got in the jeep to go down to the river for this late afternoon cruise, a band of marauding elephants came as if to attack me. They were bachelors, said the guide, young bachelors. They were bullies. The tracker claps his hand repeatedly against the jeep to make them stop and not maraud the vehicle. A bachelor elephant stormed directly towards the jeep, and the jeep retreated backwards. My days were numbered. The bachelor elephant then came around the vehicle to the side where I was sitting and started coming for me personally. This elephant was literally staring straight at me. Should I not be making direct eye contact with this elephant? I wondered. Some antipoachers in the bush beat on drums distracting him or calling him away and eventually he went off in their direction.

Our guide said he was taking some guests on a river cruise a few days earlier and another tracker called him on the radio to say a lion was killing a baby elephant somewhere nearby. The guests implored him to take them there. Oh Jonathan, they said, we have to see that. So he drove the boat back to land and took them in the jeep to where it was happening. Then while watching it they wept and said, Oh Jonathan, why did you take us here…

When we got back to the camp the staff was lined up again waving at us like Downton Abbey.

At your bedside in the safari camp inside the mosquito net is a type of horn/alarm—the housekeeper says "in case of emergency" euphemistically and does not specify what kind of emergency, but I think we all know what kind of emergency. My days are numbered.

September 8, 2023

Awoke at six a.m. to go on game drive. Our guide pointed out a herd of impalas frolicking across the way.

"The impalas are celebrating. They're not sure what they're celebrating."

Monumental mounds of elephant dung in all the roads. The landscape is so dry you think all the trees are dead.

The bachelor elephants were in a really bad mood yesterday, he told us. Elephants are emotional, they said. But the other animals are quite philosophical. The night before we left my younger daughter Grace had watched a movie called *Beast*, starring Idris Elba, who takes his daughters on a safari where they are terrorized by a lion run amok. (Just to prepare for the safari by scaring herself out of her wits.) Poachers killed the lion's family and that is why he ran amok. But in reality, the guide said, the lions see their children and family members killed all the time and they do not really repine. They know it's just how it is.

I went to the library and the gym at the camp. I met some other guests. They were funny. They also said the elephants came on their patio last evening and ate their fence. Their camp was on the river. I walked back to my villa alone and terrified since the elephants like to come down to the river; you can see the frequent evidence of their presence on this path that I was on. I wondered what actually to do if I encountered a belligerent bachelor elephant alone on my walk. Later I asked our guide. He said: Run.

Dinner in the bush with lights strung up at tables among the other guests. Our tent manager said if I encountered an angry elephant or other wild animal on the path at night to remain perfectly still. He encountered a lion on the path one night and knelt down to its eye level while emanating a mystical and somehow supplicating attitude of equality until the lion walked away.

September 9, 2023

Starting to break down. The old bones, the aging brain, the lions in the path.

I knew this trip was not for the faint of heart or the old.

We left Zimbabwe.

Sign at airport: WARNING: PERSONS MAKING INAPPROPRIATE COMMENTS, HIJACKING, CARRYING WEAPONS OR EXPLOSIVES *MAY* BE PROSECUTED.

Younger daughter Grace finally slept eight hours, though woke up at five a.m. "So I took a malaria pill and went back to sleep," she said. I'm not sure that's the way you're supposed to take the malaria pills. It's not like you just pop them at random times. Plus on the bottle it says to take them with large amounts of food.

The hotter it gets, the more turbulent is flying, and it was ninety-five degrees. We were on a tiny propeller plane. We were not allowed to bring regular suitcases because the planes are so small. We also had to put our carry-on items in the hold, so I fished out my pillbox and clutched it tightly in my hand, in case the need arose.

It arose immediately. I was sitting next to a lady from San Diego. My daughters had met her party and kept telling me how glamorous they were. I kept chatting with her desperately throughout the flight (which was severely frightening). I told her about my recent hip replacement. She marveled at my being on this trip so soon after and was incredibly supportive. I told her this was not a trip for the old, and told her how old I am. She professed shock that I was so old. Needless to say, I adored her.

When we landed I experienced huge amounts of relief and felt I could go forward. Then I found out we had to get back in the same plane and go somewhere else for an hour, plus drop people off and then get back in it to go farther after that. The supportive lady had gone off somewhere else on her glamorous trip. I took another tranquilizer but was kind of weeping quietly during the next flight, occasionally looking down (from way too high up) on the monotonous bleak landscape while bouncing around. Like there's nothing out there. I did notice one man looking at me with a kind expression so that helped.

"Where's the pilot?" I asked when we had got back in the

plane. He had to go to another job. So the copilot flew the plane for the second leg.

A lady from Chicago told us about her safari. We hear this kind of story a lot. They keep asking their guide to take them to a kill and then when they get there and see it they are sobbing. This lady saw a leopard killing an impala; then a hyena came and kicked out the leopard to eat what it had killed. Chicago lady quietly sobbing. Four leopards hissing at hyena but hyena wins out in the hierarchy. Guide asked sobbing lady if she'd like him to move on. No, I'll just sob quietly and look away.

After dropping some more people we then took off for the last leg. The last two stops were at single landing strips in the middle of nowhere.

Finally we achieved our destination and then I was in ecstasy. It was so pure. Botswana is like the Garden of Eden. It's like the Dawn of Time.

So today went from despair to ecstasy.

Even the warthogs in Botswana are incredibly charming. Everything is very distinct and pure. It's a delta, an alluvial plain, sort of like a Louisiana swampland but with incredibly non-humid clear air. Especially compared to Zimbabwe at the camp on the Zambezi River, which was foreboding, with elephants constantly crushing the dry gnarled branches.

The elephants are in a great mood in Botswana. Because they're in the Garden of Eden. You drive out in a Land Cruiser that can go on any kind of terrain including water. You just constantly plunge into water and drive through it. Because there's water everywhere.

In the evening we saw the most entrancing lioness and her cubs. The lioness was so dignified and elegant; her mischievous and adorable cubs frolicked near. She was plainly exhausted, now relaxing on the Edenic plain, while also alert and watchful of the cubs in a resigned and noble way through her exhaustion. The lioness not only looks after the cubs but also hunts the food. So she is doubly exhausted.

The head of the pride is one lion who has five wives. He has one sidekick who is a weaker smaller lion who shares his wives and helps him patrol his territory. But that seems less hard than what the female has to do. Plus the lions sleep all day. We saw the two males sleeping soundly in the marsh. Like they had been out on a binge all night. I don't know why they deserve to be the king of the jungle. They don't help with the children, they don't hunt. All they do is make sure other lions don't try any funny business with their wives.

September 10, 2023

Awakened by crashes on roof of tent, then saw cascade of baboons gamboling down the tent poles and across the porch.

They're not carnivorous so it's OK.

A baboon decided to join us for tea. He came cajoling into the tent and crashed onto the tea things. He was going for the sugar, which he began shoveling into his mouth.

Maybe it's not OK, about the baboons cascading all over the tent.

In 2019 a guest was gored by a buffalo here while walking along the path between the tents at night. He was gored in the collarbone. The girls asked if he was helicoptered out to a hospital. No, "first aid" was administered and then he was helicoptered out in the morning.

This area in Botswana is a national park operated by the government. This safari camp is owned by a couple called the Jouberts. The Jouberts wrote a book called *Relentless Enemies* (about how the animals hunt). I was reading it. In recent years the lion pride was bigger here. There was a mentally disturbed lioness who ate all the cubs. That reduced its size. Some said it was because she had no children of her own. But the Jouberts wrote about it in their book and said they could tell from her anatomical details that she had just been nursing when they saw her eat some cubs. So I'm unclear on it.

NEWSFLASH: The people who got gored by the buffalo were not random guests; it was the Jouberts, the owners, specifically Beverly Joubert. This seems ironic. They were walking from Tent 2 to the main lodge for dinner at seven p.m.—so it was barely even dark, though maybe it was raining. She was gored not only in the collarbone but also the arm and one other place. They thought she'd died four times (but she survived); her heart stopped. There was so much blood the staff could hardly handle it but took care of her all night until the helicopter came in the morning. Beverly Joubert was in her sixties when this happened. Her reaction to this horrific event was to try to make things better—for the buffaloes.

In other words, she's insane.

But also inspiring. The Jouberts are major-league conservationists, so for her it's all about making the environment better for the animals, though it already seems pretty good. It's basically the Garden of Eden. I don't know how it could get any better.

The traumatic story weighed on my mind. I read more about her. She wanted to make things better for the women of Africa too, after getting gored, and plainly the Jouberts are completely altruistic people.

Not only did she survive but she's totally good as new, the staff said. You couldn't tell anything traumatic had happened to her—except the scar. Maybe scars plural. In the lodge there was a gallery down a side hall lined by many old black-and-white photographs of the Jouberts. Jack studied them when we first arrived and had remarked that the Jouberts look like movie stars. I went to study them and thought, Wait, those *are* movie stars, aren't they? But no, they're the Jouberts.

September 12, 2023

Yesterday on the game drive we tracked a lioness who was walking slowly through the brush. The safari vehicles have been around here for decades and the animals know they are not to be feared. Still it's a little weird to be in a jeep following five feet behind a lioness and she doesn't seem to care. She walked and walked. We followed, our dear guide Mots driving over bushes in our way. Finally she came to some random bush and made a noise. Shortly two cubs came tumbling out overjoyed to see her, madly jumping all over her while she submitted to their adorable embraces. Mots said she was exhausted. As far as I can tell, all lionesses are exhausted, as they do all the work.

Probably trying to impress my millennial daughter Adelaide, I said it was so typical of the patriarchy even in the animal kingdom for the lions to take the moniker King of the Jungle when they don't seem to deserve it.

"Mom, they don't speak English; they're not the ones who came up with that."

Mots assumed the lioness was hungry. She had been out hunting all day and had told the cubs to stay in this one place till she got back. Whether she was hungry or not, the cubs were also hungry, and started nursing.

Our guide Mots is ultraprofessional but not only that. He has charisma and I have a giant crush on him. It's weird when you have a crush on people and you're old enough to be their mother. But that's how it is now, making it yet more embarrassing.

At night back in the camp you have to close all the doors and porches and stay inside. Sometimes I get tangled up in the mosquito net thrashing about.

In the morning Jack asked me if I knew what kind of animal had made a certain really big sound in the night. "Was it the grunting?" I asked. "No, I think it was the moaning." Or maybe the growling. The girls also heard some serious roaring and crying at five a.m. that went on for a while traumatizing them.

Mots came over and we had a long talk about it with Teddy, the manager of our tent.

The Jouberts have a lot of style. It's strictly an old-world style from the 1920s—Oriental rugs and mahogany floors and massive wood furniture in the tents. You expect to see a Victrola.

September 13, 2023

Yesterday my feeling for the male lions changed dramatically. We came upon the two male leaders of the pride—Mots calls them "the boys"—the big leader and his weaker sidekick. They were resting as usual but Mots could see that they were badly injured. The two lions of this pride are brothers and their wives are five sisters. The bigger lion, the main leader, was more badly injured—on the mouth, which was still bleeding, and the leg.

The weaker sidekick had scratches on his face. P.S. the weaker sidekick doesn't seem that weak.

Mots pieced together what had happened. They went out to another concession to try to expand their pride. Before my change of attitude I would have said they just wanted to look for new women to have sex with—but that shows my lack of understanding. So then I reasoned if they got a new woman they could bring her back with them to become one of their wives, who would have babies, and thus increase the pride that way.

But they were defeated out there.

Defeat is more interesting than victory. The ancient Greeks preferred to write heroic legends of defeat, which stirred men's hearts more than tales of victory. These two defeated lions stirred mine.

They were at the same time pathetic and majestic, diminished by their wounds. The weaker sidekick rolled over on his back and slept that way. The leader lay in the MGM pose looking sadly nobly in the distance.

I asked Mots would the women come and comfort them. Not really, they're too busy. Plus they seem kind of mad, like maybe the way you'd be mad if your husband had five wives, etc. But now I was no longer mad at them. They were too weak to hunt. Would the women bring them food, I asked Mots, or bring the cubs to see them. Not likely.

After a while the weaker one who was less injured hauled

himself up and slowly started walking away across the grass to somewhere. When he had gone about twenty feet he roared weakly for his brother to come along, then went on walking slowly onwards. Eventually he stopped to wait for his injured brother, who was then seen limping stoically across the grass. They were a heartbreaking pair.

Of course Adelaide kept saying I'm even more sympathetic to the patriarchy when it's hurt. That I try to learn her teachings, but then the patriarchy reels me back in when the men are wounded. She says they've been wounded by their own toxic masculinity.

Later we stopped for drinks on the Edenic plain to watch the sunset. Grace asked Mots what the other guests were like. In actuality she was fishing for compliments, the subtext of her question being kind of like, are we his favorite guests. Mots is far too professional to take the bait, maintaining the same hearty strength at whatever happens. But he did say that we were the only guests who skipped one of the game drives.

As the park is reached by driving out across a death-defying series of narrow bridges and plowing directly into various bodies of water, a fascinating but somehow arduous process—that's one reason why we skipped it; also you need time to think and write and read. We found that others in the staff were also shocked that we skipped one of the game drives. We analyzed this again amongst ourselves. "They need to know we need to read and write and think," I said.

"Yes, it's important to raise awareness about rich people and what they can do," Grace satirized me.

It's also kind of like when you're in Egypt and they keep showing you mummies and you feel like how many mummies can you really see without getting the point. Like you already do get the point. There's such a thing as seeing one too many mummies. But there is not such a thing as seeing one too many lions.

What is really the source of their dominance? Jack explained it later.

Night had fallen. There was a full moon. We followed the injured lions for a while as they slowly walked across the plain. Then headed back to camp, plowing directly through rolling swaths of water and across perilous narrow bridges in a daring night drive through the bayous, arriving back at the tents at eight p.m.

The next morning the girls were traumatized because at three a.m. they thought they heard a kill going on—roaring and crying and the "death call" Mots had described. It went on for hours. Our tent manager said it might have been hippos mating. Which sounds like buffaloes suffocating.

Mots came over and we had a long talk about it in the tent.

My attitude to the lions just changed again. I asked Mots: To make sure I have this right, the lion didn't just want to go have sex with someone new, he wanted to bring a new girl home to increase his pride. Right?

Wrong.

The lion is not going to bring a new woman home because if he tried to do that, his other wives would get really mad and definitely kick her out. So in a way the lion's quest is doomed. While scoping out the neighboring pride he may attack or be attacked by its leader who is out protecting his own territory. "A male lion is ever restless; his is an endless quest for expansion, for new females with whom to mate..."

So I asked Mots: But in the lion's *mind*, does he just want to have sex or is it more that he is nobly seeking to increase his pride.

Which is a pretty ridiculous question. Or could you ask the same question about humans? Naturally Mots looks askance sometimes instead of answering my questions. He's not a lion mind-reader. Meanwhile I'm trying to stifle my giant crush on him so it won't be embarrassing.

Jack pointed out the source of the lions' dominance when after their defeat, one was on his back sleeping heavily, oblivious to threat, despite the proof that they were not immune to it. In fact the lions' level of security and confidence is so genetically complete, sprawled out in the grass unafraid and unrepentant, as every other animal sleeps nervously, with one eye open—lions are the only animals who are NOT insecure, including humans. If humans had the confidence of lions—put it this way: when you're insecure, you have problems.

*

It was our last day. You drive in suffocating heat to the tiny airstrip ten minutes away in the jeep with all your bags. Mots makes sure the tiny airstrip is clear of animals. The tiny propeller plane is there. It is ninety-three degrees. All farewells are emotional. I felt incredibly emotional about Mots. Grace has had "anticipatory nostalgia" about the inherently gorgeous Botswana landscape since yesterday.

I wasn't scared this time in the tiny prop plane, though it made four stops before our destination (being kind of like a bus). I pretended I was flying over Africa with Denys Finch-Hatton. Also I just wasn't scared anymore, I get it, this is how you do it.

Finally we arrived at Maun, an airport in Botswana where we transferred to a regular plane for Cape Town. Then there are forms, customs, checkpoints, long lines, and it keeps getting hotter and the whole trip seems pretty hard on the old bones and I try to tell various random people how it's all kind of rugged for someone my age.

"Interesting strategy, Mom," said Adelaide. "What exactly do you hope to gain by your eccentric effusions of despair to strangers??"

Probably the sympathy I'm not getting from Adelaide.

Flying into Cape Town looked like flying into California—over mountain ranges to the sea. We had to meet our guide, which was humiliating because in the bush of course you need a guide, but I don't need a guide in a big city. Plus, you formed an emotional relationship with your guides, and I didn't have enough emotions to keep doing that every time.

But while the others have moved on to Cape Town I can still think only of the lions. I'm reading more books about their behavior.

September 14, 2023

I miss Mots.

Cape Town is a bit of a conundrum. Investors from the Emirates redid the waterfront so it's practically like Dubai. Or just anywhere, more like. The vibe at this waterfront/port area is super well-heeled, with Ferrari dealerships everywhere. No idea why or who shops there. Asked Tim, our guide. He said, Foreigners.

Tim said he was taking the King of Nigeria on a tour some years ago. The King asked him, Why is it that the Europeans are the only ones who do things here? I guess that was before the Emirates put their hand in.

Downtown a banner on a church read: THEY ACTED SHAMEFULLY YET THEY WERE NOT ASHAMED... THEREFORE THEY SHALL FALL. Our guide Tim explained he is a mixed race of European, tribal African, Indian... He is from Johannesburg. His father told him, My boy, go to Cape Town. He started out as a theology student. He loves dancing. His wife hates it. He doesn't always make sense. He's very enthusiastic. He keeps saying that everything is "next level."

Often I got yelled at by the girls for being from the previous level and the only way I finally got them to stop was one night in Cape Town when they were toting up the aspects of my obsolescence and destroying the remaining shreds of the obsolete viewpoints they believe I possess, I left the dinner table to go sit in a chair somewhere else with my glass of wine and watch the world go by. When I came back they seemed to feel some compunction that I was offended or hurt by their remarks and I said, No, I was just bored by them. You're teaching me and I do learn, I said, but sometimes it's just boring.

But I do know, they're next level and I'm previous level.

September 15, 2023

I sat on a bench at the edge of the world and framed my mind for the Cape of Good Hope which I had always wanted to see. I had always read how treacherous it was for sailing ships to navigate in old British novels; it seemed a wonder of the world. We hiked up a giant hill gazing at its sublime beauty in rapture until reaching a lighthouse with an exhibit about its history, which I could not take in because the mind is recalcitrant to absorb certain kinds of information after being focused on wild animals. Also there were some abnormal baboons on the rocks traumatizing Grace.

The next day she was felled by headache and other ailments. I hovered maternally about and ran her a bath spiked with a healing bouquet of herbs and flowers from the Winelands. Tomorrow we go back into the bush for the last safari. Worried for Grace in that respect. I don't think there are doctors nearby in the safari camps.

September 16, 2023

Tim took us to the airport, Grace still under par. Despite the healing herbs and flowers. Tim told us the safari camp we were going to is next level, but he thinks everything is next level.

I thought I knew what fear was. But I didn't. I didn't know what fear was until I saw the plane we were taking to Kruger National Park. The pilot met us at the quiet airport in the countryside and brought us to his tiny plane. It was so tiny that you felt it could be blown away by the slightest breeze. It was a four-seater. Adelaide sat up front with the pilot (who, she said later, kept checking his Instagram while flying the plane), Grace and I sat in the two middle seats, and Jack was in a kind of jump seat in the back. The flight was ultraturbulent. It was ninety-six degrees and raining. Buffeted around in the tiny vehicle. I wished we could have stayed at a low altitude as I always feel better if I can see the ground so I know what I'll be plowing into if it all goes wrong. I tried to keep looking at the ground but it was like looking into a deep bowl and Grace's side seemed less gorge-like so I looked out of hers. I gripped my seat tightly and tried to read a book about the lions.

The airstrip where we landed had an adorable thatched waiting room open to the air. Our new guide and tracker picked us up. The usual instructions to beware when walking from your tent to the lodge—but much more intense, I thought. You might step on something. You might see something. Alert the staff.

I couldn't make out exactly what the extra threat was. We'll have to worm it out of them. They did mention that three lionesses were seen by the path recently. I also saw a little card in the bedroom saying that there is a unique abundance of leopards here.

If you see something, say something. Like leopards.

It was ninety-nine degrees. The game drive started at three thirty. Secretly I wished it could start at five thirty when it might be cooler.

I waited at the lodge sitting on the deck. Looking at a snake. Coiled around a tree. It was starting to unwrap itself from the tree and inch towards me. I edged back to my room.

The landscape was much more like Zimbabwe—close dead dry gnarled branches everywhere along narrow paths. We saw a hyena and the wild dogs everyone keeps talking about which have mottled coats of yellow and black and purple. Stopped in narrow path for drinks. You'd think I'd need a drink. But I don't drink. It's all part of the anhedonia.

After dinner the porter accompanied us to our tent, where Jack insisted on getting a cigar to bring back to the lodge to smoke while having more drinks. I had to beg the porter to look out for him on his way back in a possible drunken stupor staggering through the leopard-laden night.

September 18, 2023

Awoke at 5:18 a.m. for game drive. Decided to get up and just do stuff till six thirty departure. Stuff like take a shower, which I was scared to do last night while Jack was up at the lodge smoking his cigar. This place really puts the fear of God into you. It may be the architecture. The architecture is in a brutalistic modern style that makes me nervous mentally. Then there's the hype: this is the newest lodge built around here and everyone keeps talking about how amazing it is. Also I think I'm getting a disease.

Our guide Sipo met us at the lodge, carrying a gigantic gun. Your guide always carries a gigantic gun. I'm starting to think it's just to make the customers feel safe; I asked Sipo if he ever had occasion to use his gun, he hemmed and hawed, finally admitting he would never use it. I have no idea if it makes me feel safe, though.

Sipo went off-road to track a leopard he saw, mowing over large dry gnarled trees crashing through the brambles. The leopard was pregnant so she was skittish and we did not find her. We saw the wild dogs on the prowl for game. Followed by three scary hyenas lumbering along. And a warthog.

The warthogs have way more personality in Botswana. They're so distinct and sharply drawn there, dark black against the green alluvial plain. Speaking of the green alluvial plain, I pine for it constantly. But later we stopped at Castleton, the oldest lodge here, which was more old-fashioned, with verandas seemingly graced by breeze and shade, situated on a plain with lakes. There we saw a dazzle of zebras which was strikingly exquisite. And a mammoth elephant drinking beside them on the lake.

I asked the manager to escort me to my tent along the treacherous paths when we got back and tried to worm some information out of him about what untoward drama happened here. He claimed it was just normal stuff that happens in the bush. As a last resort I asked him if he knew of the Jouberts. He did. He said that Beverly Joubert had been gored again. I found this hard to believe. Surely this altruistic woman couldn't just go from place to place trying to help the buffaloes and then getting gored by them.

That afternoon we finally saw a pride of lions here. But no

one in this region is interested in the lions—guides, trackers, staff—all they care about is leopards. Our tracker had a book in the vehicle with photographs of all the leopards in the area, and capsule biographies of them. He showed it to us page by page describing each one lovingly while we were parked beside the lions. Do you have a book about the lions? I asked then. No. Why not? I asked. They all look alike, he said dismissively. Which Adelaide said was racist.

I guess I liked it when there was a clear-cut hierarchy (or patriarchy?) of which the lions were the undisputed king, so I guess I am the dingbat patriarchy upholder as usual.

The lions were being very social—two males, two females, and two cubs—all together in a thicket. We were watching two cubs madly nursing at one of the females. The other female's cubs had been killed. When a lioness loses her cubs in that manner, she immediately goes into heat, so the lioness who had lost her cubs was pregnant.

Adelaide skipped the next evening game drive and was sitting on the porch at the lodge. Someone called Sipo to tell him that there was a hyena and some wild dogs eating an impala from that viewpoint at the lodge. Those remaining at the lodge amounted to Adelaide and the staff. So she must have seen the famous kill that everyone wants to see. We asked her if she did. She said she tried to block it out.

A porter came to escort us down the paths to dinner. Like most of the staff, he's from around here. Trying to make conversation I said, So you're human and you live constantly amongst wild animals who are dangerous and that's how it is and you're used to it and you observe it and you know how to do it and you like it and . . . I rambled on eventually concluding my statement and he said, YES!

September 20, 2023

Some inane person, which I think was me, suggested that we take a game *walk* instead of the game *drive* on our last evening. Coming upon a small dry plain that looked sort of like the British countryside if there was a violently serious drought, we disembarked and Sipo loaded his gigantic gun. We marveled at his gun and asked him a lot of questions about it. He said we must walk single file so that if a snake came it would get him first. Or at least he would see it first, then set forth on a highly unpleasant walk over parched thickets clotted with elephant and antelope dung, the dry brush crackling under every step.

Whose idea was this? I wondered. Oh yeah, mine.

After about a mile I remarked I saw the road and Sipo politely led us back to it. Soon the tracker showed up with the back of the vehicle set up for the sundowner, pouring champagne. Grace asked her usual question about were the other guests obnoxious. A surprising recital of the sad and obnoxious behavior of other guests ensued. They sit in the far back of the vehicle checking their cell phones and not talking to him and it's very trying and the three days he spends with them seem like a sad eternity. Are they American, I asked. Sipo tactfully claimed that they were not. The obnoxious guests were Mexican, Chinese, or European. Meanwhile Grace's questions got more and more far-fetched. Has anyone ever broken up or gotten divorced while you're taking them on a game drive? She asked. A seemingly ridiculous question. But the answer was Yes. And it seemed believable because of how Sipo described it. Grace piped up, So they're fighting in the back and you're like: Um, there's a leopard on the right?

I did see some obnoxious Americans at the lodge demanding that they see a cheetah and that they see it kill something. Why is everyone so bloodthirsty, I wondered. Plus it's the law of the jungle, you can't plan that or demand it at your whim.

The end was near. And it's not pretty. It comes abruptly. I was fading. I had been fighting off a disease since helping Grace with her vivid headache and congestion in Cape Town. I tried to stay calm but it turned out to be COVID, on the two revolting Emirates flights (eight hours and then fourteen hours) home. My throat felt like razor blades and I could not swallow. On the horrendous endless flights. Dubai is out of the way and it's only because the Emirates captured the market on the route to Africa in a capitalistic way that we go through there. I hate them now.

The Emirates. Or maybe just being on a plane for twenty-two hours is not a good place to be when your throat feels like it has razor blades in it.

I tried to focus only on the lions, having read more about their behavior. Maybe it has to do with my misbegotten embrace of the patriarchy, my misbegotten understanding of the world in the effort to adapt. But if the meek shall inherit the earth, at least I'm standing near the front of the line to inherit the earth.

My quest to understand the lions and their open challenge to the world continued. "Deep down I suspect," wrote the author—"it is not scientifically proven but I believe it to be true—every male lion who loses a pride and a territory and even one who has never ruled a pride, still, until his dying day, yearns for power."

The drama escalates. If you're looking for drama you don't need the ancient Greeks. You don't need Shakespeare. All you need is lions.

"Males will usually team up with brothers or cousins to form a coalition. Occasionally, unrelated males will join together," as in one pride observed, led by two lions who formerly had been archenemies. In his youth one had killed the other's father. So they had been lifelong adversaries dedicated to revenge. It would be poetic to say that no one knows why they joined forces, these old foes turned allies. But we do know why. The reason was necessity. "And after one of them was killed, the other roamed the forest for nights roaring, calling for his friend."

With special thanks to Emily Stokes

NANCY LEMANN was born in New Orleans and is the author of six books, including *Lives of the Saints* (available as an NYRB Classic), *The Ritz of the Bayou* (republished in 2026 by Hub City Press), and *Malaise*.

Praise for *Grandfamilies*

"*Grandfamilies* is a moving, compassionate, and indispensable read, both a tribute to the strength of carers and the children they've raised and a call to action for policymakers to support grandfamilies with the resources they need and deserve."

—Debra Whitman, PhD, author of *The Second Fifty*

"Donna Butts has painted a picture of resilience, fortitude, and hope. *Grandfamilies* inspires action to ensure that all children have the nurturing care they deserve by supporting all families, reinforcing caring communities, and providing public policies that recognize that caring for each other is a collective responsibility."

—Joan Lombardi, PhD, senior scholar and adjunct professor at the Thrive Center for Children, Families, and Communities and author of *Time to Care: Redesigning Child Care to Promote Education, Support Families, and Build Communities*

"This is a book that has readable and understandable strategies, information, solutions, and insights that are useful to members of kinship, grandfamilies, service providers, and policymakers. In one book, the author has consolidated the lived experiences from caregivers, the grandfamily triad, and extended family, as well as current knowledge and research from experts in the field. A must-read."

—Dr. Joseph Crumbley, LCSW, global kinship care expert and author of *Relatives Raising Children: An Overview of Kinship Care*

"Saving a child is the work of angels. This book is full of souls being saved—children and grandparents. Donna Butts writes of her angel's hand lifting up souls and lifting every reader."

—Juan Williams, journalist and *New York Times* best-selling author of *New Prize for These Eyes*

"*Grandfamilies* lifts up the voices of grandparents and kin caregivers who step in with courage and love when children need them most. Their stories remind us what is possible when we choose to invest in families instead of leaving them to navigate alone. This book is both a powerful testament and a call to action for anyone who believes we must do better by caregivers and the children whose futures depend on them."

—Ramsey Alwin, President and CEO, National Council on Aging

"Donna's passionate call to action for grandfamilies simultaneously recounts the journeys of relative caregivers and of those advocating for them. While celebrating the considerable progress made, it also highlights the work that remains in reforming a social safety net that largely ignores or erects hurdles for grandfamilies to access support."

—Rob Geen, child welfare expert and editor of *Kinship Care: Making the Most of a Valuable Resource*

"Donna Butts is America's leading voice on the power of intergenerational connection and collaboration. In this wise, compelling, and beautifully written book, she draws on decades of insight and experience to bring to life the role grandfamilies are playing in the lives of children, older people, and the communities they are helping to heal and hold together. *Grandfamilies* is essential reading for anyone interested in the changing shape of our social fabric, and the promise of our multigenerational future."

—Marc Freedman, founder and co-CEO of CoGenerate and author of *How to Live Forever*